I0619870

BERING SEA TERROR

BY
MATTHEW NEFFERDORF

SEVEREDPRESS

BERING SEA TERROR

Copyright © 2024 Matthew Nefferdorf

WWW.SEVEREDPRESS.COM

ISBN: 978-1-923165-21-2

PROLOGUE:

The creature swayed in the water like a ghost in the darkness, observing its surroundings for prey that was on the move. It enjoyed hunting in this new land it had discovered, the prey was abundant, and no predators dared approach a monster of its size. Small crustations moved in groups below, just waiting to be caught and devoured by the new terror of the Bering Sea. With tentacles spanning over 100 feet in length, it reached with ease and scooped dozens of crabs at a time, shoveling the small creatures into its massive beak. While this species of prey was incredibly small, they made up for it with a whole ocean of them.

The water was ice cold; it was used to cold temperatures from living in the depths of the ocean, but this water held blocks of ice on the surface. The only way to keep its body warm was to eat as much food as possible. The cold, at times, drove it into madness. While the Opilio crabs it devoured had a delicious taste, they did little to quench the growing hunger of the giant cephalopod. The life of this creature had been set into two cycles, sleeping, and hunting. While there was other prey to chase, they were scarce and used too much energy for such a little reward.

It finished eating the large biomass of crabs and began swimming in search of more sustenance. Being the Apex predator of the Bering Sea, the creature swam with ease and without fear of any foe in the water; in its previous home, this was not the case at all. Every day was a fight for survival and required constant guard from the other monsters of the ocean, it battled fifty-foot sperm whales, sharks that traveled in packs, and even its own kind. After a life of death, carnage, and bloodlust, the monster embarked on a journey in search of a new home, where it could kill and eat with ease.

While a life of ease was appealing to the creature, that did not mean it did not wield the capabilities to kill any creature that stood in its way. Aside from the one-hundred-foot cobra-like tentacles it used to crush any animal that stood in its way, it wielded a beak that was as sharp as a razor and was capable of biting clean through the back of a blue whale. Feeding on the crustations became a simple matter of scooping armfuls into its mouth and savoring the sweet flavor.

The hunger inside of it grew, driving the aggressive nature of the beast to unimaginative levels. It swam as fast as it possibly could to look for any kind of food that would satisfy the hunger that drove it to near insanity. Suddenly, it spotted something resting on the sea floor, something large that it had never encountered before but could only be one thing: Food. It moved cautiously towards the strange food source, expecting at any time to be attacked. Swimming within half a tentacle length from the object, it snaked one of the smaller tentacles down and pulled the strange animal to its observing three-foot eye.

It quickly realized that this was not food at all, this was a trap used to catch other creatures, such as the crustations it enjoyed feeding on. While this would hold an easy banquet of food to quench the hunger, this trap was empty; energy had been spent with no reward at all for the colossal squid. Feeling the anger increase to a level that was borderline demonic, it transferred the trap to its longer arms and flung it straight down to the floor as hard as it could. The trap exploded into hundreds of pieces, scattering over two hundred yards away. Powered by madness, the squid bolted away as fast as it possibly could, scanning every inch of the ocean floor looking for food, but finding nothing.

CHAPTER ONE:

Captain Tom Wilder walked down the pier for possibly his last season running his boat; he couldn't take another fishing trip like his last one. A two-month King Crab fishing season panned out to be his worst trip in his thirty-year career; instead of catching the boat's quota of eight hundred thousand pounds, his boat scraped by with a mere sixty thousand pounds. Barely enough money was made to pay for the fuel they had used to venture out for the season. Paying the crew had been a nightmare and Tom had to resort to selling anything extra that was on the boat, including the spare radio and life raft.

It had been over twenty years since he took a loan out from the bank and bought his boat named *The Restless*. Spanning one hundred and fifty feet long and weighing over four hundred tons, she was one of the biggest ships in the crab fleet. While she had been neglected over the years on the sea, causing rust to form from bow to stern on the outside, she possessed exactly what the captain needed to make his living. During calm seas he could carry a load of one hundred and eighty crab pots, which proved why the boat was named *The Restless*, his crew rarely slept during a trip with how busy he kept them.

As he got closer to the boat, he felt a light finger tapping on his shoulder. Turning around to see his deckhand, Tommy Mitchell; none of his gear was with him.

"Hey Cap, everything about ready to head underway for the new season?" Mitchell asked nervously.

"If you were down here with the rest of the guys, you'd know how much work still needs be done before we can leave this shithole," Captain Wilder replied angrily.

Mitchell looked down at his feet and contemplated if he had the courage to tell the captain what he came here to say, but he could tell he was already in a bad mood. Their boat was the laughingstock of the entire harbor, coming in last in terms of the final crab count, but it was not for a lack of trying. No matter where they dumped their stings of pots, it was like the crab had simply disappeared. Staying up for days at a time, eating almost no food, and then coming back to harbor to be handed a check for a couple thousand dollars was starting to be more than Mitchell could take. To make matters worse he was the ship's diver so any time a problem for the boat involved going into the water, he was the only one qualified to put on his dive gear and go in.

He snapped back into reality when he heard Captain Wilder yell at him, "I know exactly why you don't have your gear and why you're letting all the others bust their asses while you're nowhere to be seen! You had a bad season so now you want to put your tail between your legs and quit, but you're too much of a pussy to even say it."

Mitchell snapped, "I've busted my ass for you for years and we always made less than all the other boats. Last season was the worst we've ever had, I've got bills that I'm behind on and all I got for my work last season was a two-thousand-dollar check and better luck next season. So, excuse me if I want to find someplace where I can make some money and have an opportunity!"

Anger rose in Wilder's eyes when he heard the word "opportunity" come from Mitchell's mouth. Aside from his poor work ethic and constant complaining, Mitchell's past was one that nearly cost him his livelihood. "If I were you, I wouldn't complain about not having an opportunity again, since I'm the only reason you even have a job and are not living on the streets." Tom stepped closer to Mitchell and pointed his finger into his shoulder. "I seem to remember a strung-out junkie walking along the pier crying like a girl because no one would hire him. I took the risk of giving you a job and put my license on the line while you got clean. So, don't ever talk to me about wanting a fucking opportunity, you hear me? I gave you one and you did nothing but piss it away."

Mitchell felt like he had just been punched in the gut, but he knew the captain was right. If it wasn't for Captain Wilder, Mitchell probably would have died on the streets because of his addiction. Walking around the town, high, looking for where he would get his next fix and looking for a job to earn some money. He stumbled to *The Restless* and begged the captain for a job on his boat, informing him he was a certified diver. Wilder had needed a diver on his boat for years, but they were hard to come by; once he checked Mitchell's credentials, he gave him an ultimatum: Go to rehab and get clean for the coming season or keep living on the streets and see how long he lasted.

"I'm sorry. You've helped me more than anyone else has, Cap, I appreciate everything you've done for me and for giving me this job. But I need to bring in money, I'm behind on my bills and I don't want to lose everything and end up back where I was."

"You think you're the only one with bills that you have to pay?" Captain Wilder responded. "I'm responsible for more bills than you can imagine but I still found a way for you all to at least walk away with something last season. So, either get your shit and get on the boat so you can make some money or turn around and never come on this boat again, Mitchell."

He looked behind the captain and stared at the boat: another two months of back-breaking work with little food or sleep and possibly another horrible payday. But that boat was the only option he had right now. "My gear's in my truck, I'll go get it and meet you on the boat, Captain Wilder," Mitchell replied.

"Good, don't take too long," Wilder shot back, and finished his walk down the pier to *The Restless*.

******

The boat was a hive of activity; much work needed to be done before the start of the Opilio crab season could begin. On deck, Deck Boss Mike Caden oversaw the madness. Having been Captain Wilder's right-hand man for more than twenty years, he knew what they needed to do even if the captain wasn't there. At the age of forty-five years old, he was the second oldest crewmember on the boat, only beaten by

Captain Wilder. After over twenty years of being on the rough seas, his five-foot-ten body was beaten beyond belief. Even with his body torn apart by waves and more than fifteen bones in his body broken, he was still able to keep up with the best of them.

Mike yelled to the newest member of their boat, Greenhorn Kyle Thomas, "Hey Greenhorn, make sure we have enough bait stowed away for this trip! That's gonna be your whole job while we're out, cut, gut, and bait the pots!"

"My name's Kyle, but I'll make sure we have enough, boss," Kyle replied.

"First of all, your name is whatever we say it is; until you earn your stripes, it's Greenhorn. Second, without bait we ain't gonna catch shit when we get out to the fishing grounds. I've never left port without enough bait for the season and I'm not gonna start now because of a newbie like you. Got it?" Mike asked.

"Got it, Mike, I didn't mean anything by it," Kyle replied. "I just don't want to fuck up and make the captain regret bringing me on the boat."

Mike looked at him and gave him the best advice he could. "Look kid, follow three rules and you'll be just fine. Number one: Do your job the way it needs to be done. Number Two: Keep your mouth shut and don't talk back. Number Three: Make it to port without going overboard. You follow those rules and you'll be just fine."

"Ok," Kyle said as he checked the bait hold and realized they were going to need much more bait than he thought.

Just as Mike finished moving the crab pots into position with the boat's hydraulic crane, he spotted Travis Marcam, the boat's hook thrower, come out from the crew quarters and begin making sure the crab pots were all tied together and secured for the trip. Being it was the month of January in the Bering Sea, they could expect to have waves that could reach over fifty feet high and winds blowing over thirty knots an hour; the last thing the crew needed was to have pots crashing around on deck and killing one of them.

Travis, sitting at a staggering 6'1, was one of the strongest men in the fleet. While he spent most of his spare time in the gym, he was considered one of the best hook throwers in the fleet, only missing the pot a handful of times in his career. While injuries are common out at sea, Travis felt the enduring pain the Bering Sea had to offer when a hook from the hydraulic crane came loose, smashing him in the face. To the surprise of the entire crew, he stood up, blood and teeth pouring from his mouth, and continued hauling the remaining pots in the string.

"Hey Mike," Travis yelled. "How many more pots do we have left to load up?"

"We got about fifteen more. Go in the galley and ask Harvey how it's going with getting all the food loaded up," Mike instructed from the hydraulic controls, not taking his eyes off the moving pot.

Travis walked off the deck and entered the galley to see Harvey Bowens, the ship's cook, loading canned food into a cabinet. "How goes it, Master Chef?" Travis asked. A short, bald, pudgy man turned around and gave a grin that reminded Travis of looking at a Jack O Lantern. "Not too bad there, Travis, just about done stocking the galley and I'll be up in a few minutes to give you all a hand. You hungry, by the way?" Harvey asked eagerly.

Rolling his eyes, Travis gave him a firm "no" and walked back outside. While Harvey was one of the nicest men he'd ever met, it drove everyone insane when every encounter ended with him trying to cook them something. While the food was always good, many times it had to be left on the galley table because they had work to do and that put them in an even colder, bitter mood.

******

Captain Wilder stepped over the boat rail and finally put his boots down on the deck, feeling the solid wood of the deck boards under his feet. He took a big breath of the salty air and felt a snowflake hit his face; a storm was beginning to come in. Turning, he saw Mike set the last pot down on deck and walked over to greet the busy crewman.

"Hey boss, good to see ya." Mike waved from the controls. "We should be ready to leave in about two hours. Have you seen Mitchell, by chance? He hasn't shown up and we've been working a man short all day."

"He'll be here soon. Son of a bitch tried to ditch us the day we're supposed to leave. I don't even know why I keep giving that guy chances," Captain Wilder growled. "All he does is complain about money and try and skate out of work whenever possible."

"But he's here when it counts, and he has saved our asses quite a few times with his diving gear. Not to mention you don't see too many people that choose to get sober in this industry and stay sober," Mike answered the irritated captain. "And you can't completely blame the guy with being concerned about being paid, boss."

"What's that supposed to mean, Mike?!" Wilder snapped back.

"Nothing upsetting, Tom, just that times are hard, so I understand why he'd consider leaving. After the season we just had, I'm surprised he's the only one that considered leaving."

Wilder could feel his face start to redden and the veins around his eyes start to swell. "Whose fucking side are you on? I put money in your hands even when there wasn't any, just to make sure everyone got a little bit of something!"

"Woah, take it easy, Cap, I didn't mean it like that." Mike walked from the crane with his hands up. "I've been with you since I started this job and we've had our fair share of bad years and I still stayed by your side. And everyone decided to stay this year too, we're all on your side but you have to try and be a little understanding, especially to the younger guys."

"I'm heading to the wheelhouse; I need to make sure all the systems are in the green for us so we can get out of here," Tom answered and walked to the rear of the boat where his captain's chair was.

******

Taking a seat, he observed the tools he used for his trade: Steering, throttles, his Global Positioning Unit, and his computer with his map overlay where he could input where he had set his strings. Taking his hat off, he scratched his head and massaged his eyes; he knew Mike was right. Driving his crew hard was one thing but kicking them while they were down was one of the lowest things he could do to them. Even after everything, they still stayed. Captain Wilder looked out the window and saw Mitchell climb onto the boat, duffle bag in hand.

Wilder needed this season to pan out, he had to find the crab and there was no one on the boat to find them but him. Looking at his charts from his previous declining seasons, there was no way there was going to be any Opilio crab where he usually fished at. Knowing the other captains in the fleet, they were all going to be fishing in the same spot and trying to set strings there would be a nightmare. In a feat of desperation, Tom looked to the Northwest end of his charts, and debated if he dared go to the place where almost no fisherman returned from. He grabbed the mic for the ship's intercom. "I need everyone in the galley in five minutes, I have something to discuss with you before we head off."

CHAPTER TWO:

The galley of the ship was in desperate need of renovation, but it possessed everything the crew would need to keep themselves fed or become a place for a quick nap. Aside from the basic appliances such as a stove, microwave, and sink, Captain Wilder had installed a top of the line walk in freezer, allowing the crew to stay out longer than any other boat. On a usual trip, Harvey kept the freezer stocked with everything from beef roasts to frozen pizzas; while he preferred to make all the meals from scratch, a quick frozen meal was better than letting a prepared meal go to waste.

Walking from the freezer to the pantry, Harvey looked inside to make sure the final bit of food was packed away. The floor was stacked with boxes upon boxes of potatoes, loaves of bread, and 5lb bags of rice. Looking to the shelves, he observed the rows of canned food and condiments that lined the pantry. Feeling satisfied that there was enough food to feed an army, he closed the door and took a seat at the table with the rest of the crew.

Sitting next to Harvey was Justin Ganks, recently promoted from greenhorn to deckhand, a decision that had mixed feelings with the crew. While Justin had been a 'Horn' for three years, he still made mistakes that were usually made by year one rookies. His youthful age didn't help matters, being he was only twenty-one years old, and he had the appearance a strong wind would blow him right over the deck.

To his left was John Hagar, who knew every inch of the boat and served as the engineer for over ten years. John was a man that had motor oil for blood and could fix anything that could break on the boat. The running joke on the boat was that he was part machine with how well he understood mechanical problems.

Mitchell walked in and sat down across from Harvey, next to Kyle and Travis, while Mike stood next to the sink in preparation for the news from the captain. "Anyone want me to make a quick snack before he gets here?" Harvey excitedly asked the men as he stood up.

Mike piped up, "For Pete's sake, sit down, Harvey. Cap will be in here any minute and he doesn't need you stuffing your face while he's talking. By the tone of his voice, I'd say this meeting is about something serious."

Captain Wilder walked in as Harvey sat back down, the air instantly going cold as they anticipated what this was all about. He walked to the table and looked around the room, eying every one of them before giving the news that could potentially cause him to lose his whole crew.

"We had a shitty season last month, and we've been having worse ones as the years have been going on. Some of you may think I've lost my touch at finding the crab but that's not the case. I don't know if it's from so much fishing over the last few years or we did something to piss off the sea gods, but the crab simply aren't here," he informed them, no one daring to say anything about his abilities.

"I've been looking at the charts and I think I have found where we can go to fish. Following the fleet and trying to set pots there will be a nightmare and we won't have a chance with how slow we drive. Our only other choice is to go North, far North..."

Mike's face instantly dropped as he considered if he was right about what the captain was suggesting. "You think heading up to Haven Point up North is where they gonna be at, boss?" Mike asked, hoping that was what he meant.

"Farther North, Mike," Wilder answered to Mike's regret.

Travis brought his hands to his eyes and began rubbing them when he realized what the captain was proposing, and it was potentially suicidal. "You're talking about heading to the Devil's Fishery, aren't you?" asked Travis. All heads but Mike's dropped into their hands once reality set in; they could be fishing in the Arctic version of hell.

"We don't have a choice, men, we're out of options for places to find crab. No one's fished there for over five years so it's completely untouched ground and that's where we can make our big payday," Wilder said, trying to convince them.

Mitchell was the only one with the courage to say what was on his mind. "There's a reason it's been untouched, Cap. Everyone that's gone up there in the last twenty years never came back. Tyler Carring took his boat up there six years ago and they were never seen again. It was unreal, it's like they dropped off the face of the Earth."

"There could be a thousand reasons why they didn't come back, the weather up there is horrible since it's a hair shy of the Russian border and there's no one to communicate with if something happens. Not to mention Tyler took a boat with only two seasoned vets and the rest greenhorns so you can do the math on that one," Wilder replied. "The only weak link we're gonna have is Kyle, but as long as you keep your head in the bait station and don't stab yourself, we should be fine. But anyone that doesn't want to go needs to say so now."

No one said a word for a minute. Engineer John Hagar finally broke the silence. "You know what scares me the most, Cap?"

Captain Wilder looked into his eyes and asked, "What's that, John?"

Meeting his gaze, John replied, "In ten years, you've never given us a choice to leave once we were on the boat... until now."

For once, Captain Wilder didn't know what to say. He knew exactly what he was asking them to do and could feel the eyes of all of them staring at him, awaiting his response. He was asking them to participate on the most dangerous trip any of them, including himself, could possibly imagine. He let the crew see a side of him he had never let one of his fellow fishermen see: empathy. "Maybe because I know exactly what I am asking from all of you, and what the possible outcomes are. But mark my words, when we make it back to port, and we will make it back to port, they're gonna be talking about us in every bar from here to New York City."

The crew still had an unsure look on their faces, but it wasn't a look of defeat. Wilder could tell they were weighing the options, especially the possibility of fame from simply going on a fishing trip. He turned to look at his go-to person and deck boss, and saw him staring right at him, a look of disappointment and shock in his eyes. Wilder turned back to the crew and gave them the final order. "If you don't want to stay, you need to have your stuff off the boat in half an hour and I'll sail with who I have left. That's all, gentlemen. I'll be in the wheelhouse."

******

Tom Wilder walked back into his wheelhouse and sat down, letting the adrenaline he felt from giving his crew the news finally fade away. Taking a cigarette from his shirt pocket he put it to his lips and lit it with his flip lighter and took a long slow drag. How many would stay for the trip, if any? he wondered as he let the smoke exhale from his lungs and felt the small relief it brought him. Normally he would think to himself that he needed to quit this habit because it could kill him, but thinking about where he would be going, a cigarette was the least of his worries.

A noise broke him from his thoughts, and he turned to see Mike walking up from the steps that led to his domain, and he knew it was about the news he had given. Tom took another drag from his cigarette before putting the butt out in the ash tray. "How many want to leave, Mike?"

"None," Mike muttered back to him. "What the hell are you thinking, Tom? The Devil's Fishery? We're not that desperate, man. There are other places where we can go to, and we can make a decent catch for some money."

Tom pulled another cigarette out and lit it. "Wow, maybe you're right about the crew being loyal ... And yes Mike, we are that desperate. This is gonna be my last season out there. I owe you all a fortune before I hang up my hat and I need to have a little something to put back into the boat. I can't leave you a piece of shit boat after always being by my side all these years."

Mike had a look of confusion on his face, and asked, "What do you mean leave me the boat?"

"Who else would I trust to be in charge once I'm gone?" Tom asked. "You're more than ready, Mike. You're a natural leader, you know every job on this boat, and after letting you set some strings, you'll know what to look for to find crab."

"I don't know what to say. You're not just saying that because of where we're going, are you?" Mike asked.

Tom chuckled as he put his cigarette out. "No Mike, no matter where we fish, this boat is going to you, and this is my last season. But I want you to have a better start at being a captain than I had when I took these throttles at the helm."

Mike stood in shock as he realized his dreams of becoming the captain of a crab boat would become a reality. After working for so long he managed to forget what he wanted most: to be the man at the helm that could change the fate of his fellow crew member.

"What do you say, Mike? You got one more trip with me in ya?" the seasoned captain asked while extending his hand.

Mike grabbed his hand and shook it. "Always, Tom."

CHAPTER THREE:

The boat slowly made its way out of port, a full crew in her galley and empty tanks waiting to be filled. Pulling out at fourteen knots, it would take the crew seven days to get to the Devil's Fishery. That time would be filled with the most sleep the crew would get in one sitting for the rest of the trip. Soon, they would be working off three to four hours of sleep while staying awake for possibly thirty-six hours.

Mike paced the deck in anticipation, going over every inch of the boat to look for any preparations they may have missed for the trip. Once he found they were all set, he walked down to the engine room in the bowels of the ship and found John looking over the engine.

"How's she running?" Mike asked him, hoping for good news.

Wiping his hands on a towel, John turned and shook his head. "We should have put more money into the engines, Mike. She's running ok right now, but I'm worried we might end up blowing a head gasket with how hard we're gonna be pushing them just to make it there. We were supposed to have done an overhaul, but it never happened."

Great, Mike thought, already the bad news was starting. "Just do the best you can, John, and keep an eye on it every spare second you have."

John gave a salute to his crewmate. "You got it, boss."

Mike walked up the stairs and made his way to the wheelhouse to deliver the bad news to the captain.

He walked in to see Captain Wilder drinking a cup of coffee and looking at his computer screen which displayed the fishing grounds they were heading to. Wilder's eye twitched with concentration as he selected the best spots in which to lay his strings of crab pots.

"Hey Tom," Mike interrupted. "We got some potentially bad news."

Without looking from his computer screen, Captain Wilder brought his coffee mug to his mouth. "Tell me about it. I've been looking at these charts and they haven't been updated in years. Just one more thing to make this trip even more difficult."

As the bad news added up, Mike sighed as he gave his news. "John thinks the left engine might take a shit on this trip. He's afraid of how hard it's gonna be working that it might blow a head gasket, and if that happens while we're in bad weather out there we'll be screwed."

Setting his mug down, Tom took his baseball cap off, scratched his head and closed his eyes, before answering. "We got two engines so we should be fine. Tell John to keep an eye on it and feed it as much oil as she needs. The money we make from this trip we can probably buy a whole new engine."

Frowning at the lack of concern for the engines, Mike did what a good deck boss does, and did as his captain said.

******

After five days traveling at sea, the crew was beginning to feel cooped up in their quarters inside the ship. There were four separate rooms where they slept and thought about life back in town. Three of the rooms held two small beds and were a little bigger than an oversized bathroom. The fourth room belonged to Mike, who had the privilege of having a room to himself. While it was smaller than the others, it made a significant difference having a space that solely belonged to him and could get some time to himself. But that time would soon be coming to an end as the fishing grounds grew closer.

******

Stirring from his bed, Mike rubbed his eyes and looked at his watch, 7:15am, time to get the rest of the boys up and start getting the equipment ready for fishing. He grabbed his pair of jeans and put on a white t shirt before heading into the galley. Harvey was already at the stove cooking a large breakfast of scrambled eggs and bacon for the crew. The aroma of fried pork filled the whole ship as Mike poured a cup of coffee and sat at the table.

"I wasn't expecting anyone else to be up already or I would have had everything ready for ya," Harvey said as he put some bread into the toaster.

Mike nursed his coffee as he attempted to wake up from too much sleep. "It's ok, man, I'd rather wait to eat with the guys anyways. Can I ask you something, Harvey?"

Stirring the eggs and adding some shredded cheese to them, Harvey turned to him. "Yeah, what's up, Mike?"

"Why do you work on a crab boat? Cooking is your life, and it seems like you really enjoy it, why not get a job that's safer, like open a little diner or something?" Mike asked him with a sympathetic look on his face. "Have the freedom to cook all day long without the risk of getting your foot caught in the pot rope and going over the side."

Harvey stood there for a minute and thought about it. Finally, he smiled and answered, "I like cooking for people that appreciate it, people like you guys. You all bust your ass out there in negative degree weather for days at a time. I'm not the best help when it comes to being on deck, but at least I can make a good hot meal for you when you're able to eat. I'd rather be out here than anywhere else."

Mike would never understand how a man like Harvey, the nicest man he had ever met, had survived this long in this line of work. He never seemed to let anything get him down and always had a smile on his face, especially when serving a plate piled high with food. The door to one of the quarters opened and out stepped Travis, wearing nothing but a pair of grey sweatpants and hair that was more cowlick than anything. John followed behind him and both men went straight to the coffee maker and poured a cup.

"How'd you ladies sleep last night?" Mike asked them as they sat down across from him.

"Ehhh," John remarked. "This guy was snoring all night, I about took my blanket and slept out on the deck."

Travis lit a cigarette and blew the smoke out. "It ain't my fault the boat makes me sleep really hard. I'm trying to get every last minute of sleep I can before we start this shindig."

"Well, that ended when you woke up today, Travis. After breakfast we have to start getting those pots untied and prepped with bait and line so we can start dropping them. We have less than two days and a lot of work to be done," Mike informed him.

Without missing a beat at the mention of work, Harvey came to the table with three plates piled with eggs, bacon, and toast. "Here ya go, guys, the others can eat when they finally wake up. Anyone need some Tabasco sauce or anything?"

Travis put his cigarette out in the ashtray and stared hungrily at the plate set in front of him. Breakfast was his favorite meal of the day, and his ideal meal was classic eggs and bacon. "You sure know how to start the day off right, Harv, this should set us up pretty well for the day."

Mike looked at his plate and felt his stomach growl; he was going to miss having the ability to sit down and eat three square meals a day. "Don't get used to the food either, man, that's the next thing to go once that first pot goes in the water."

Travis gave a sad look on his face as he savored his first bite. "Yeah, I know. I just wish we could eat like how we work, nonstop. I'd trade food over sleep any day."

Mike tried his best to throw him a bone. "I'll see if I can put a word in the captain's ear about making more time for food. This trip is gonna be our most dangerous one yet so the least I can do is try to make sure you all have the energy to stay alert."

"You'd do that for us, Mike? I appreciate that, man!" Travis rejoiced, nearly knocking over John's coffee with his hands.

"Hey, easy, man!" John yelled as he moved his cup away from Travis. "So we may get a little more food, big deal. I'd take sleep over food any day, or an engine that won't shit the bed at any second."

Mike laughed as he looked at John and explained, "I can't do anything about the sleep or the engine, but you'll have a full stomach to complain about both."

Harvey came over with a pan filled with more eggs. "Anyone want any more? The rest of the guys are coming out now."

******

The hull of *The Restless* rocked up and down as it battled against the waves, the sun hidden by clouds and rain, water splashing over the deck rail and covering the crew. Finally in the waters of the Devil's Fishery, the weather made a clear point to make these men work for every crab they caught. While it was January there was no snow yet, but the dark skies indicated to them it would soon be arriving.

The crew hustled to remove the chains and binders off the remaining crab pots and not to fall into the deathly cold sea. Captain Wilder watched the crew on his outdated surveillance camera to keep an eye and make sure everyone was always accounted for. Working on the stack of pots was one of the most dangerous jobs on the boat, one slip and you were gone into the freezing ocean.

Justin Ganks crawled on his hands and knees on the top of the stack, about ten feet in front of the window of the wheelhouse and thirty feet above the deck. Nervously, Justin crawled and started loosening the last binder attached to the pot. Suddenly, the boat pitched to the left as a wave crashed over the right side and Justin started to roll towards the end of the stack as he lost his balance. At the last second, he managed to grab hold of the pot netting and stop himself from falling overboard. His body shook from shock; five more feet and he would have rolled over the side.

Captain Wilder did his best to correct the boat with his rudder controls and was able to level it out so Justin could regain his footing. Grabbing the intercom, Mike pressed the talk button, "Sorry Justin, get that last binder off and get the fuck off the stack. It's getting bad out there and it's only gonna get worse."

"No shit it's bad out here," Justin thought to himself as he unfastened the binder and began climbing his way down the stack. "I almost rolled off the side because you couldn't keep control of the boat."

Feet finally hitting the deck, Justin walked over to Mike and addressed his concerns. "This is ridiculous, Mike. We're supposed to start dropping pots tomorrow and already I almost fell off the boat. This weather is too shitty to be working in."

A wave crashed over the side of the boat and pelted the crew with daggers of ice-cold water. Even with waterproof coveralls on, it did nothing to stop the water from hitting their faces and running down their backs. Mike gave a shiver as he spat out seawater and looked at Justin. "I don't want to hear you bitching already about the weather when we've only been working for a few days. Get your ass back to work and stop whining."

"Alright," Justin answered as he walked across the deck to help Mitchell with tying up any holes in the pot lacings that they could see.

Mike leaned against the wall at the bait station and took a cigarette from his coveralls and lit it. Already he had people complaining. Shockingly, one that wasn't was Kyle, the greenhorn. The kid didn't know much about fishing, but he did exactly what he was asked to do, and he learned fast; faster than Justin ever did. Mike watched as Kyle inspected the grey colored lines used to attach the pots to the buoys. The young fisherman scoured over every inch of the line and made sure there were no cuts in them. A cut rope meant they could lose the 800lb crab pot as it was hoisted up and could cost as much as 1,000 dollars to replace.

Inhaling the smoke, Mike heard the intercom speaker next to him, "How's the kid doing?"

Smiling, Mike answered the captain. "Not too bad, boss. I'm not gonna say I'm impressed but I've seen a lot worse. Haven't heard him bitch or complain once so far and he's been looking at that line like it asked him on a date."

Captain Wilder chuckled through the speaker. "Good, keep him busy and make sure he doesn't cut any corners. As soon as you guys finish up, Mike, get everyone inside. It's gonna get worse out there and there shouldn't be more left to do until tomorrow. I want everyone to get one more night of decent sleep before the grind tomorrow."

Shocked, Mike mumbled into the speaker, "Uh, yeah, you got it, Cap. The guys will be happy to hear that."

"They better enjoy it; tomorrow we drop our first pot, and the weather should be better. We'll be doing at least twenty-four hours straight," he answered the deck boss.

"Now we're talking!" Mike answered cheerfully.

"Harvey's making a special dinner tonight too, pot roast and potatoes, with some cheesecake for dessert," Captain Wilder informed him.

"I thought I smelled something other than sweaty ass and WD-40 out here. Sounds like an inmate's last meal though, Tom," Mike laughed.

For the second time today, Mike heard a chuckle from the salty captain. "Let's hope it's not, Mike. Have Mitchell and Kyle check the block over and that should be the last thing before getting that bait cut up tomorrow. Once that's done, you guys come inside and call it a day."

"Yes Sir!!" Mike yelled.

******

Kyle was exhausted already but didn't dare let the others see or hear it, that was a sure way to get on the wrong side of the crew and be left without a job at the end of the season, if they made it back. The last of the pot line was finally checked and only a handful had to be replaced. As Kyle stood up to look for another job, Mike walked up to him.

"I need you to go with Mitchell and check that the block is in working order and then we're done for today."

"What's a block?" Kyle asked, confused.

Mike realized how much this kid had to learn. "It's the wheel-looking device hanging over the side of the boat that the pot line goes in to haul the crab pot from the bottom. Without that thing, we can't haul our gear. Mitchell will know what to do but just make sure it's in working order."

Kyle gave him a nod as he walked to find Mitchell and finish his work. Another wave splashed over the deck and a river of water rushed under his feet, dropping him onto the deck. Embarrassed, he picked himself up as Harvey came out from the confines of the boat and walked straight towards him. In his hands was a large ham and cheese sandwich. Stomach grumbling, Kyle realized he hadn't eaten in over 8 hours. Harvey thrust the sandwich into his hand.

"Eat it quick, before the captain sees you!" Harvey yelled as the wind whipped around the boat. "I'll try to bring you guys out food as much as I can this season but no promises.

Captain Wilder gets really pissed when food gets put before hauling our gear!"

Kyle ate the sandwich in three bites, it was the best sandwich he had ever eaten. Layers of ham, smoked gouda, lettuce, and mustard; Harvey was able to turn a simple snack into a meal fit for a king. "Thank you, Harvey!"

Harvey gave him a pudgy smile. "No problem, kid. Keep your head up, you're doing great!" With that, Harvey walked back into the ship, away from the freezing weather and rolling waves.

Kyle turned and saw Mitchell looking over the device that Mike described as the block. Walking over to him, Kyle had to yell to talk above the roar of the wind. "What do you need me to do, Mitchell?"

Mitchell turned the block on and watched as the wheel rotated, looking into the grooves in the middle of the wheel where the line sat and saw no defect in the metal.

"Nothing now, it looks like she's running fine," Mitchel answered.

"How does this thing work?" Kyle asked him.

"Long story short, when Travis throws that hook and catches the line between the two crab pot buoys, he'll pull the hook back in and put the buoy line in this block. Mike will turn it on, and it'll spin and pull the line and the crab pot up from the bottom. Once the pot's on the surface, Mike will run the hydraulic crane and pick the pot up with the crane hook and seat it into the pot launcher. After that he'll activate the hooks on the launcher called dogs that hold the pot in place. Once all that's done, we can tilt the pot towards the deck, open the door, and hopefully be sorting a lot of crab," Mitchell explained to him.

Kyle gave him a deer in the headlights look. "That sounds really complicated."

Mitchell shook his head. "It's simple and you'll get used to it after a few pots. But you'll be at the bait station so leave this hunk of metal alone. You'll probably just get yourself hurt. Let's head inside now, I'm tired of being wet."

Mitchell and Kyle informed Mike that the block was in working order. Mike gave the news to the captain that everything was completed.

"Get your asses inside now and get dry!" Captain Wilder yelled into the intercom. "Dinner is just about ready."

* * * * * *

Food was again on the squid's mind, its eye continually searching for more of the small crustations to feast on. The tentacles flowed behind the monster as it sucked in water and jetted it out behind it, causing the squid to propel forward. Food was beginning to become less plentiful in this drying oasis. The need for feeding was becoming too much for the squid as it found itself eating more than sleeping.

Suddenly, it spotted a small biomass of crab moving below it. The small mountain of legs and claws detected a predator lurking about. The mass started to crawl away at a faster pace; the squid couldn't let this chance for a meal get away. Shooting down, the squid swung its two massive fighting tentacles together into the cluster, smashing dozens of crabs together. It opened its razor-sharp beak and began shoveling the crab into its mouth. Once inside, the force of the beak sliced through the shell of the crabs with ease, turning them into mulch before being swallowed.

The feeding went on for over ten minutes and not a single crab was able to escape the insatiable appetite of the one hundred and thirty foot killing machine. A single Opilio crab attempted to flee while the others were being eaten. The crab made it ten feet from the group before a tentacle wrapped around its body and within a second, was crushed into a pile of shell and guts. The squid quickly brought the flesh to its mouth and feasted on the tiny creature that tried to deny it its nourishment.

The warmth slowly returned to the squid now as it drifted with the current, allowing the meal to digest. Rest would soon become the next priority, and then it would begin to search for food again.

The squid could feel something else was in the ocean with it, something large that it had never encountered before. The senses of the squid couldn't find exactly where this new creature was, but it knew it was far enough away to not be a threat at the moment. Once sleep was achieved, it would scout and find this new creature that was trespassing in its territory.

With luck, it would become the next meal and would provide enough nourishment to last the squid for days.

Allowing its body to simply drift with the current of the Bering Sea, the squid was finally able to rest and recharge the energy it would need for the coming day. While there would be no dreams, it was able to think of the coming hunt before sleep overtook this nightmare of the sea.

CHAPTER FOUR:

The sun rose above the sea the next morning; the storm had finally passed to reveal sun rays of warmth that was ideal weather for fishing. The sea was calm, and the boat rocked gently as it made its way to the location where they would set their first string of pots. The crew was already up and sitting in the ready room after they had finished putting on their waterproof coveralls and gloves. While the room stunk of cigarettes and the propane heaters that ran continuously, it was a little haven they could go into to get ready and walk right out onto the deck. If necessary, the men could walk into the room from outside between strings and catch a quick nap or simply have a seat for a few minutes.

Captain Wilder got little sleep during the night; he couldn't shake the feeling of anticipation that he always felt the night before he laid his first pots. Normally he would set out only a couple of pots and see if there was crab in the area, but this time he was going to lay half of his pots here, and then travel west and lay the other half. This was a very bold and potentially disastrous idea, but if it paid off, it would set them off strong for the season. Being untouched ground, his chances of getting full pots of crab were better than they would be in his old fishing grounds.

Wilder grabbed his intercom mic. "Alright guys, time to get to work."

The crew threw half lit cigarettes down as they left the ready room and ran to their positions to start setting their string of ninety pots. Kyle chose to walk instead, and was corrected by Mike on what speed he should be performing at, "You never walk on this boat! Unless you are heading to your rack, everything is done at a run, Greenhorn!!"

Kyle ran to the bait station and began putting the small blocks of frozen sardines into the bait machine and watched as it turned it into a chunky mulch. He scooped the mixture into a rectangular container filled with holes that would be strung up in the pot to help attract the crab and flood the ocean with the smell of oily fish. Next, he grabbed three whole cod fish that would be strung up in the pot as well and become food for any crab that was trapped in the pot. By the end of the trip, Kyle would have processed over two thousand pounds of frozen fish and whole cod.

Meanwhile, Mike was at the hydraulic station where he ran the controls for the crane, the block, and dogs on the launcher. Using the controls, he picked up the first pot and carefully hoisted and moved it over the top of the pot launcher. As he slowly lowered the pot down, Mitchell and Travis stood on both sides of the pot and assisted seating it into the launcher.

Once it was secured, the two crew members unfastened the gate at the bottom of the pot to open it up, pulling out the line and buoys. Travis grabbed the line and threw it on top of the pot while Mitchell took the buoys and prepared to throw them over the rail when the pot was launched. Kyle rushed forward once they were clear and jumped into the pot, hooking the container and cod fish in the middle of the roof.

After climbing out, Kyle helped Travis in closing the gate and tying it off. Once that was finished, Mike gave Captain Wilder a thumbs up to announce the pot was ready to go over the rail. The boat's horn blared quickly, which signaled the men to launch. Mike hit the button and raised the launcher up, causing the one-thousand-pound crab pot to dump in the ocean with an enormous splash. Kyle started to walk in front of Mitchell who was about to throw the buoys over, but was forcefully pushed to the ground by John, causing him to fall onto his back. Mitchell scooted his feet towards the rail and first threw one buoy and then the second, completing the process of dropping a crab pot.

John stood over Kyle and began yelling, "You never walk around the line when a pot is going over, you understand me!? Especially in front of the guy that's throwing the damn buoys over!!"

Kyle could feel his anger rising from being pushed to the ground like a toddler. "I'm sorry but you didn't need to push me like that, asshole!"

John bent down and pulled him up with both hands and thrust him against the side of a crab pot. "I did because you were about to get your foot caught in the line as it went over. You think you can outmuscle an eight hundred pound pot? I just saved your life, so shut up and get back to chopping bait, Greenhorn!"

Letting go of him, John lit a cigarette and walked away, heading to prepare the next pot to go into the ocean.

Captain Wilder watched from above at the conflict going on. He grabbed the hand mic and asked Mike what was going on.

"The newbie about walked into the line as the pot was going over and almost got his foot caught. John saved him, a little aggressively, but saved him from going over the side," Mike informed him.

Captain Wilder growled back into the mic, "Damn fool, make sure he knows how to walk around when pots are going over. And keep him at the bait station, Mike! I don't need someone going over the rail on the first day out here!!" Tom slammed the mike down, already steaming over how long their first pot took to launch, too slow for his timeline.

"You got it, boss," Mike promised.

******

Kyle sulked his way back to his bait station, still irate about being pushed around when he had been working his ass off.

"One fucking mistake and he thinks he can just do whatever he wants to me," Kyle muttered as he prepared the bait for the next pot.

"Kyle, get over here!"

Kyle looked up to see the deck boss staring at him and ran to the hydraulic controls. Mike didn't look happy, and he knew it was about what had just occurred. The first day of actual fishing and already hands were being put on crewmates; not a great way to start the season.

"Sometime today you need to thank John for saving your life, if you haven't done that already," Mike informed him.

Looking down, Kyle thought of what to say. Finally, he answered, "I haven't yet, but I will in a little bit. He didn't need to push me to the ground like that though, man."

Mike used the controls to move the next pot into place. "Actually kid, he did. If Mitchell had thrown that buoy, one more step and that line would have wrapped around your foot and that pot would have dragged you to the bottom. You'd be crab food before you hit the seabed."

Not realizing how close he had been to death, Kyle felt embarrassed for getting so upset at the guy that had gone out of his way to keep him from drowning. "I didn't know..." Kyle mumbled while staring at his feet.

"If your foot ever gets caught in the line, you drop to your ass and lay back. It might help your foot slip out and it will buy us some time to come over with a knife and cut the line. So, he put you in the saftest position as fast as possible by pushing you down," Mike informed him as the next pot was laid on the launcher.

"I'll be sure to tell him thanks and apologize for being an ass to him, man," Kyle reassured Mike.

"Where's the fucking bait at!!?" a voice yelled from the crab pot.

Kyle ran back to his station and grabbed the next container and cod fish and ran to the pot, hooking them inside. Getting out of the way, Kyle secured the gate and walked behind Mitchell this time, as the pot disappeared into the sea and the buoys were thrown.

Turning to see John crouched at the next pot, he walked over and prayed he would accept his apology. "Hey John."

John looked up from unfastening the next pot to see the greenhorn standing above him. "What do you need?" John asked coldly.

"I just wanted to say thanks for saving my life, and I'm sorry for being an ass to ya. I didn't realize what you did until Mike told me," Kyle explained.

"Don't thank me, man, we all look out for each other on the boat. I've seen a guy go overboard that way years ago, and you don't forget something like that. We heard him screaming for help and by the time we got to him with a knife, the pot pulled him over the side," John explained morbidly.

"Guy had a wife and two kids, didn't even have a body to bring back for them to mourn. So, always keep your head on your shoulders and look at what's going on around you. Everything on this boat can kill you, always remember that."

"I will," Kyle answered.

Suddenly, the voice of the captain echoed through the deck, "If you do not get that fucking pot ready and dropped in the water, I'm gonna lose my fucking mind!! You all need to pick up the pace or you can forget about even thinking of the word sleep!!"

The crew hustled back to their stations and began the marathon of work that would be filled with nothing but agonizing labor, immense hunger, and the hope that all of this would pay off in the coming days.

******

Captain Wilder rubbed his eyes and could feel the sleep that was attempting to overtake him. The crew had been up for over seventeen hours and now they were in the process of setting the last pot. The whole crew was beyond exhausted, but surprisingly the one with the most energy was the greenhorn, still going at a running pace. He couldn't say the same for Mitchell or Justin, who appeared to be shuffling everywhere they went. Even Mike was beginning to slow down and had made a couple of close calls with the crane, almost swinging it into Travis.

This was the most dangerous part of fishing, working when the body was past the point of needing sleep. Mistakes were easy to make when your only thought was about your bed and a hot meal instead of the job at hand. Captain Wilder had been driving them hard all day and night, but the end was approaching soon. He looked out and saw Mike give him the thumbs up and for the last time tonight, Captain Wilder blared the horn and watched the pot go over the side.

He grabbed the mic and gave the news the crew had been waiting for all night long, "That's it for tonight, guys, come on in and get some sleep. Justin, you're on first watch tonight and then Mitchell. Don't fall asleep when you're in my chair or you can find another job."

The crew stumbled back into the ship and made their way to their rooms while Justin poured himself a cup of coffee and went to relieve the captain.

******

Looking behind him, Captain Wilder saw the door open, and Justin walked through, an irritated look on his face.

"She's on autopilot, so don't touch anything. Make sure we don't run into any rogue waves and keep an eye on the weather, might be changing in a few hours. Don't fall asleep either. You need me I'll be in my quarters," the captain uttered.

Justin sat down in the chair and slammed his coffee down and began mouthing off, "Why is it I always have first watch after we've been working all day and night? Why don't you make the new kid do it? He's still full of energy and he's the lowest man on the totem pole."

Tom could feel his face become flush with anger; no one talked back to the captain of the ship. "Why don't you shut the fuck up, Justin, and just do what you're fucking told!?"

Justin's face became as red as an apple as he bit his tongue before saying something that would cost him his job.

"The reason the greenhorn isn't doing watch is because do you honestly think I would trust someone that has never crab fished before to know what to look for when being up here?" he yelled. "And second, I'm sick of the complaining and poor attitude from you, I haven't heard the greenhorn complain once since we've been out here but that's all I hear from you!"

Justin sat there and clenched his fist around his burning coffee mug, scalding his hand but not letting go. "I work just as much as everyone else and I'm tired of being treated like a piece of shit by everyone."

"Then stop acting like a piece of shit! It's that simple! Do your job, keep your mouth shut, and actually earn your money. If we have to have another conversation like this again, I'm gonna give your share to Kyle. The way he's working, you're the one that deserves a flat rate instead of a percentage of our quota." With that, Captain Wilder walked out of the wheelhouse.

Justin vented to himself about what he had just been told; it was the most infuriating conversation he had ever had with the captain. "Who the fuck is he to say that piece of shit is gonna get my share," he uttered under his breath as he drank from his cup. "I did my time getting yelled at, treated like shit, and doing the bitch work for the whole crew, now it's his turn."

He looked to make sure no one was around and pulled a small bottle of whiskey from his coveralls. He poured a finger of the brown liquid into his cup and let the smell hit his nostrils before taking a sip. If he was gonna be up for another four more hours he might as well be comfortable. Drinking on a boat at sea was against every rule and ethic of fishing but screw it, he thought to himself. Kicking his feet up, Justin put his arms behind his head and prepared for an even longer night.

******

Kyle stumbled his way to the galley to get a bite to eat before going to his bed. He was beyond tired; he had never worked so hard in his life. Walking to the fridge he pulled out the leftovers of pot roast from the other night and cut a piece off. Putting the beef between some bread he made a quick sandwich that would quench his hunger until Harvey made breakfast for them in the morning.

Walking to his room with his sandwich in his hand, he swayed to either side as the boat rocked; the seas were beginning to become rough again. He opened the door to his room and collapsed into his bed. Normally, he shared this room with Justin but since he was on watch, Kyle would be able to fall asleep in peace by himself. He laid in bed and finished eating his sandwich, debating if this was the job that he wanted to spend the next who knows how many years doing. After the last bite was down his throat, he could feel his eyes droop and he quickly faded off into sleep.

******

Kyle woke to the light being turned on and a shadowy figure standing in the doorway, hanging onto the door frame, and leaning to one side. His eyes adjusted and he could make out the face of Justin, who was looking back at him but appeared he couldn't focus.

"Sooooo, you think you can just come here and take my money, you piece of shit?" Justin slurred as he stumbled into the room.

Kyle looked at him with sleepy and confused eyes. "What are you talking about, Justin? Take what money?"

Justin pulled out the bottle of whiskey from his pocket and took a shot from the bottle. Wincing from the burn, he continued, "The captain said he's gonna give you my money, and I have to have your money since you're sooooo good of a worker."

Rubbing his eyes, Kyle tried to make sense of what was going on. "You're not making sense, dude... are you drunk?"

"Maybe I am, why the fuck do you care? You're the captain's pet apparently and I'm just the piece of shit that works on this boat." Justin took another sip from his bottle as it slipped from his hand, pouring onto the floor. "Fuck, well, there goes the rest of that."

"I think you should head to bed and sleep it off, man. No one needs to know this happened and you can just start fresh tomorrow," Kyle tried to reason with him.

"I think we should settle this right now; I'll show you why I'm a full share guy." Justin cocked his arm back to throw a punch and slipped on the liquor spilt on the floor, sending a loud crash through the crew quarters.

Mike stepped out of his room in sweatpants and no shirt, rubbing the sleep from his eyes. "What the fuck is going on?! We got off deck four hours ago, you guys should be getting some sleep."

As soon as the words left his mouth, the smell of booze hit Mike's nose. "That smell better not be what I think it is..."

He looked at Kyle first who looked more confused than anything, but when he looked at Justin, he could see the bottle of whiskey lying next to him. Mike grabbed Justin by his coveralls and threw him against the wall, Justin looking terrified as the drunk feeling quickly left him.

"If you ever bring that shit on board again, I will personally tie you to the next crab pot and send it over the side, you stupid sack of shit! You know the rules, no drinking on the boat, EVER!"

Mike stared at him with fire in his eyes and his hands began shaking while holding onto him. He quickly let the drunk man go before he threw a punch of his own at him. "Get the fuck in your bed and if I hear anything else come out of your mouth, you're fired and you're not gonna get a cent from this trip."

Justin climbed into his bed and stared at the ceiling, feeling the room starting to spin. "I'm sorry Mike, I just got pissed off at some bad news, man."

Mike glared at him. "This was your one freebie, no more chances after this. Get your shit straight and start being a deckhand for once in your life."

Shutting off the light, Mike slammed the door behind him. He made his way back to his room and sat in his bed. Problems like this were never good to have on a boat, especially after the first day of setting gear. Having struggled with drinking in the past, Mike understood some men had a tough time coping without it, but he never thought of bringing it on a boat. That could endanger the life of everyone else, especially realizing Justin had to have been drinking while he was on watch.

He'd give Justin this one chance and keep an eye on him from here on out. Any more slip ups and he would have to tell Captain Wilder about what was going on, but he prayed it wouldn't come to that. Justin wasn't the worst deckhand he'd seen; his biggest problem was he was young and still had a lot to learn. Shutting the light off, he thought about what the bad news could have been that would get Justin so upset, as his eyes closed to go to sleep.

CHAPTER FIVE:

Captain Wilder sat up in his bed and looked at his clock sitting on the desk next to him, 10 am; he had overslept. He pulled the blanket off and walked to the sink to splash some water on his face. Looking in the mirror, it became more apparent that this life was not meant for him much longer. Suddenly, a coughing spat came over him, making him double over into the sink and forcing his eyes to shut from the excruciating pain.

After five minutes, he was finally able to stop coughing and looked down into the sink; blood covered the bottom. The blood had come from his lungs, a lifetime of smoking over two packs of cigarettes a day. He turned on the water and splashed it into his face before rinsing out the blood.

The visit to the doctor the year before had been one of the worst days of his life. Having a painful cough for years, he finally decided to have it looked at and the results were his worst fears. The cancer had formed in his lungs and was slowly spreading throughout his body; smoking had finally caught up with him and now he was paying the price. The rest of the crew didn't know about his condition, not even Mike, and he intended to keep it that way.

Over a year of constant medical bills had depleted almost every single dollar the sick captain had, forcing him to sell everything he had at his house. Adding to his list of problems, the slow fishing failed to replenish his bank account while the stack of hospital bills continued to pile up. But this season, that was all going to change.

Grabbing the towel off the rack next to him, Tom wiped his face, returned to his room, and finished getting dressed for the day. Walking out into the galley, he stifled a cough as he saw Harvey preparing food for the day of work.

"Hey Cap, I got your coffee ready, and I made a sausage and egg sandwich for you to take up to the wheelhouse," Harvey said, handing the plate to the aging captain.

Captain Wilder quickly grabbed the plate and coffee and rushed up to the wheelhouse. "Thanks, Harv."

"Uh, no problem, sir," Harvey replied with a look of confusion at the captain rushing away so quickly.

"Hmmm, must be eager to start fishing," he thought to himself.

******

Tom walked into his workstation and saw Mitchell sitting in the chair, staring off in a daze.

"Mitchell!" Tom yelled.

Snapping out of his trance, Mitchell jumped out of the seat and stood up. "I'm awake!" he yelled.

Tom looked at him and made a disgusted look. "Yeah, I can see that. What's been happening out there since you've been on watch?"

"Oh, not a whole lot, still on autopilot and the ship hasn't sunk yet so it's been a pretty easy night. We should be at our next spot to set pots in about two hours at this speed, boss," Mitchell told him eagerly.

"Good, we can get the rest of these pots laid out and... What the hell?!?!" Captain Wilder yelled in shock as he looked out the window.

A freezing storm had passed over the boat while the crew had been asleep and covered the boat in a thick layer of ice. Ice was the nightmare of any boat on the sea, especially one that still had over half its pots on board. If enough ice formed on the crab pots that were still on board, it could cause the boat to sway to one side from too much weight and cause the boat to roll over. Dozens of boats and crew had perished due to the frozen water and the only way to remove it was manual labor and sledgehammers.

"Don't you think you should have woken me up when you saw that there was ice forming on the boat, Mitchell?!" the captain asked him angrily.

"Well, I wasn't sure what I was supposed to do, I thought it would blow over quick and we wouldn't have to worry about it," Mitchell replied.

Wilder angrily ran his hands through his hair as he looked at the condition of his boat, a solid white color instead of its usual blue and black paint job. "Obviously it didn't blow over, you idiot. If I didn't have enough to worry about, now I have to get all this ice off before we capsize over, and by I, I mean you guys!"

Mitchell looked down at his feet; another mistake, this time a big one, one that could have put the boat and everyone on it in danger. "I'll let the guys know and we'll get out there ASAP, boss."

"Finally, now we're thinking with our head. I want that ice off ten minutes ago. With some luck we can get it off right at the time we need to start dropping pots. Now get out of here and get to work," Captain Wilder demanded.

Mitchell walked out of the wheelhouse and went to inform the others of what was happening. As soon as he made it to the galley and looked at the buffet of food everyone was enjoying, the captain's voice sounded through the boat, "Breakfast is canceled, ladies! We got about three inches of ice on the boat; you have ten minutes to be out there with hammers or I'll throw every piece of food overboard!"

The men groaned as their plates went to the trash can, most only half eaten and some completely full. There were whispers coming from all of them, venting their frustrations to themselves with the start of their day.

Harvey looked with disappointment as the fruits of his labor sat in the trash, two hours of work for nothing. "I'll try and get you all some food before you start laying pots, I'll do a coffee refill here soon and bring it out to you guys."

Mike was the last one to leave the galley and turned to look at Harvey. "How about instead of cooking you come grab a hammer and start helping us. You've gotten to stay in the kitchen the whole trip so far, it's time you got some sun," Mike chuckled.

"Yeah, why not," Harvey replied after thinking it over. "I think it would boost the guys' spirits to see the dedicated cook out there chopping ice. You care if I get the coffee going before I head out there, Mike?"

"Yeah, that's fine," Mike answered. "The way this day is going, that coffee pot is gonna need to be running all day long."

******

Mike walked through the ready room and opened the door to the outside and saw his worst nightmare; there was not a single inch of the boat that didn't have a thick layer of white covering it. John walked over and handed him a ten-pound sledgehammer. Mike gave him a nod after taking it and walked to the front of the boat which was unoccupied. Giving a swing with all his might, a five-pound block of ice fell off the rail and onto the deck.

The boat rocked to the left and the ice block slid across to one of the openings on the deck and fell into the ocean. One swing down, thousands more to go. Looking across the deck, Mike noticed Kyle swinging his hammer at one of the support poles in the middle of the deck that was frozen solid. Large clumps of ice clung around the lines connected at the top of it.

"Hey, Kyle!" Mike yelled to him.

Kyle looked up before taking his next swing. "Yeah?"

"I'd clear away from the bottom as soon as you hit that pole! All that ice at the top will come down on your head if you don't! That'd be a hell of a way to die!!" Mike informed him.

No sooner had Kyle hit the pole again, a twenty-pound ice block sped towards his head from the top of the pole, missing it by a foot. Kyle jumped as he heard a solid thud behind him and realized firsthand what Mike had tried to warn him about.

Just then, the door to the ready room opened again and out walked Harvey, his coveralls barely fitting his hefty body. Everyone on deck was surprised to see the ship's cook out here, especially to do manual labor. Harvey walked over to Kyle and put his hand on his shoulder.

"I'll take it from here, kid, spots like this can be pretty dangerous, especially if you've never cleared ice before," Harvey told him.

Kyle gave him a smile and he walked away to find a safer place to clear away ice. "Thanks, Harvey, I appreciate it."

Mike heard the exchange and came over to the pole. "You know, the kid isn't ever gonna learn how to do the job if everyone does it for him every time it gets dangerous."

Harvey had a big grin on his face as he began hitting the pole and dodging the falling ice. "Oh come, on Mike, we don't need the kid dying on his first trip out. Plus, from what I've seen he's got a surprisingly good head on his shoulders for being as young as he is."

Mike groaned as Harvey attempted to undermine him. "Just get the ice off the boat, leave the kid to us, and let's get this load of pots in the water."

Harvey have him a salute. "You got it, boss!"

Harvey continued to swing his hammer at the ice as Mike walked off to see how the rest of the crew were doing. Travis and Justin had taken quite a bit of ice off the pots already while Mitchell and John were clearing the ice sitting on the deck. With the progress they were making, this ice would be gone in no time.

Mike looked up at the sky and felt a shiver as the cold breeze flew into his jacket; it must have been well below freezing right now. His eyes fell to the ocean, surprisingly calm for having a storm blown past mere hours ago. Thinking of the future and what it held for him, he couldn't help but smile as he lit a cigarette and leaned against the bait station. Soon, all this was going to be his, and he would have to make a choice on who would be the new deck boss.

While he thought Travis would make a great choice in a few years, he still had some things to learn about being in charge on a boat. The only real option was John, a great engineer and as smart as they come. The plus side was Mike had worked with John a long time and they had a great working relationship together.

Mike took a drag from his cigarette and slowly blew the smoke out; a seagull flew overhead. He watched it fly away and he wondered to himself where it would land, if it was heading home or looking for a new one. Seeing this side of nature made him think of how lucky he was to work a job like this, he got to see a side of the world few men got the chance to see.

"I'm not paying you to stand there and smoke, Mike..." a voice informed him from behind.

Mike jumped, nearly dropping his cigarette. He turned around and realized he was standing next to the intercom speaker.

"Sorry, boss, I got caught up in the view, won't happen again," Mike apologized as he picked up his sledgehammer.

"I have enough guys slacking off and I don't need you to be one of them. You're supposed to be setting an example out there," Captain Wilder growled.

Just then, Mike spotted Justin, who was having a challenging time walking on deck; he stumbled and almost fell face first, clearly still feeling the effects from earlier this morning.

Mike grunted as he spoke into the speaker, "I have something I have to address, Tom; I'll make sure we get this ice off ASAP."

Justin was still stumbling as Mike walked up behind him and grabbed his coveralls, preventing him from falling to the deck. Holding onto the railing, Justin took a deep breath as he felt his head pound and the rising urge to vomit. Before he could do anything more, he threw his head over the railing and emptied his entire stomach into the Bering Sea. Mike shook his head in disappointment and anger as he watched the deckhand spend the next five minutes feeding the crabs with his vomit.

"How much did you fucking drink last night, Justin?" Mike asked him as his head came back into view.

Justin covered his eyes with his hand to try and block out some of the sun. "Shit I don't know, too much though, Mike. I feel like my head is being crushed like a beer can right now."

"No shit too much, one drop was too much, being where you're at." Mike could feel himself getting angry again. "Now you're stumbling around like an idiot, and I can still smell that stuff on your breath."

Justin turned and threw up another load over the side and wiped his mouth. "Well, I was planning on getting a few more hours of sleep today but the ice had a different plan for me, I guess." Justin spat over the rail and began tapping at the ice like a child using a toy hammer.

Before Mike could lash out at him, John rushed over and addressed a major problem to the deck boss. "Hey Mike, we got a big problem, man!"

"What's up?" Mike asked him.

"We got a shit ton of ice buildup on the block, but I'm afraid to start knocking it with the hammer 'cause it might bust it off," John explained.

Mike thought to himself of the best way to get the ice off without breaking the equipment. "Take Travis, get the welding torch, and melt the ice off with it. But be careful 'cause that thing will melt through that metal if you hold it in one spot too long."

"Fuck, ok. We're gonna have to haul one of those big bottles of acetylene too, this is gonna be a pain in the ass," John replied.

"It's the only thing we can do though, man. Just get it done," Mike directed.

******

Down in the engine room, John went to the corner and found their stash of acetylene bottles that were secured by rachet straps to the wall. He told Travis to start loosening the straps so he could grab one of the one-hundred-and-sixty-pound bottles after he went to find the welder.

John scoured every inch of the engine room looking for the welder, finally finding it at the opposite end to the acetylene tanks. Pulling with all his might, he slid the large welding torch across the floor, but stopped when he looked at the pressure gauge to their number two engine. The gauge was hovering dangerously close to the red; the added weight from the ice was pushing the engines too hard. He had to get this torch on deck and get the rest of the ice off.

Finally sliding the torch to the base of the steps to the deck, John had just enough time to see Travis remove the last strap as the boat rolled to the left, causing one of the bottles to crash to the floor. Travis held the rest of the bottles in place as he tried to reattach the strap as the bottle on the floor rolled towards John.

"Damnit, Travis! Be careful with those bottles, they're highly flammable!" John yelled.

Travis shot him a look of irritation as he tightened the straps and was assured the remaining bottles were secure. "No shit, John, I know that! The fucking boat rolled, there's no way I can stop that bottle by myself, it's gonna take both of us just to carry the damn thing!"

John picked up one end of the bottle as Travis walked over and lifted the other end; they would have to make a second trip for the torch. "Holy shit, this thing's heavy!" Travis strained as they slowly walked up the stairs to the ready room. "How many bottles do we have of this stuff, John?"

John was red in the face as his feet cleared the last step. "We should have about thirty bottles down there; you know how often shit breaks on this boat. Plus, there isn't much a welder or torch won't fix, the hard part is trying to do it in these crazy seas."

Travis finally cleared his end into the ready room and begged John to set it down. Carefully, both men set the bottle of flammable gas on the ground while they took a couple of deep breaths.

Leaning against the wall, Travis felt like his arms were going to fall off, feeling them burn from the weight of the acetylene.

"Don't you spend most of your time in the gym when we're not at sea, man?" John chuckled.

"Yeah, I do, smartass," Travis shot back. "There's a difference between lifting weights and carrying dead weight up a flight of stairs, no one trains for stuff like that."

"Maybe you should start," John snickered as he bent down and lifted his end up again as Travis picked up his and they walked out onto the deck.

Now, the real challenge was about to begin, carrying this much weight on a slippery, ice-covered deck. Taking baby steps, the two men worked their way to the block and slowly set it down, making sure it wouldn't roll away while they went and grabbed the welding torch from the engine room.

Once back, Travis connected the acetylene bottle to the welder while John turned on the gas and connected the welder to the power. Igniting the torch, John put on his welding goggles and slowly began raking the three-thousand-degree flame over the ice-covered block, being careful not to leave the flame in one spot for too long. The ice began to melt, revealing the metal components that hid underneath.

Travis looked over to Mike and gave him a thumbs up, indicating that the plan was working. Within five minutes, the ice was completely removed from the metal and the block was perfectly intact. Finishing the job, John turned off the gas and disconnected the torch while Travis began scooting the welder towards the ready room to put it back into the engine room, awaiting John's help.

After the dangerous job of putting the welder and tank back down into the engine room was completed, the deckhand and engineer returned to the deck and continued removing the rest of the ice attached to the boat. John headed back where no one had been to yet and began knocking ice off while Travis cleared the remaining pots on deck. Using a combination of brute force and precision, he began knocking the ice off the pots, being careful not to damage them in the process.

Mike conducted a walk around to see how the crew was coming along, and to give the captain a status report on the ice removal. Much of it was already off thanks to the men working without any breaks. They would have it completely cleared well before the boat reached the next area to set pots. Walking over to the speaker, Mike informed Captain Wilder of what he considered to be good news.

"Hey boss, the way it's going we're gonna have all the ice off in about one more hour. The guys have done a kickass job and busted their asses," Mike informed him.

"This wouldn't have even been a problem if whoever on watch would have let me know that we had ice starting to form up. Now we've lost time we could be using to get the rest of our gear ready," Tom asserted into his microphone.

Mike couldn't let the captain grind the crew down to nothing after having worked hard to keep the boat safe. "I understand that, Cap, but there's nothing we can do about that now. I think the guys deserve a few minutes to get warm and get something into their stomachs before we start grinding our last string."

"Are you giving me orders, Mike?" Tom asked.

"No sir, just giving you my opinion, nothing more," Mike replied.

"Fine, as soon as the ice is all off, have them come inside. I'll call down to Harvey and have him whip something up for the boys and make some fresh coffee."

"Thanks man, they'll really appreciate that. I think it would be good to start the string on a positive note too. Again, just my opinion." Mike smiled.

Captain Wilder took a second before giving him a reply, "Make sure they're working hard when you all get back on deck, that way we can head back to the other string and start hauling the gear back on. Those pots should have a nice soak on them and with some luck, they'll be full to the brim."

"Don't worry, I'll make sure they bust their asses to make up for the food and break," Mike laughed.

"That's the deck boss I know!" Captain Wilder cheered.

******

Down in the galley, Harvey was doing his daily cleaning of the galley after helping clear ice off the deck. This boat became dirty fast when there were so many people on board and the last thing on their minds was making sure the counters were wiped down. Personally, he enjoyed the peace of mind knowing the crew could come in after a long shift of laying or setting pots and have a clean place to eat at. Even if they didn't notice it, it was his duty to give them his best while they were giving theirs.

Suddenly, the phone in the galley rang, and Harvey quickly walked to answer it. "Harvey's Kitchen, what you want?"

On the other end, Captain Wilder wasn't amused with the phone greeting. "This is the captain, Harvey. Who else do you think would be calling you on the phone?"

"Hey Cap, can I get you anything to eat while you're up in the wheelhouse?" Harvey quickly asked.

"Don't worry about me, the guys are gonna finish clearing the ice and then I'm gonna have them come in and get something to eat before we start laying the next string. See if you can fix something up for them that'll stick with 'em for a while and give them some energy," the captain requested.

"Well, we still have some of that roast from a few nights ago in the fridge, I can slice it up and make some quick mash potatoes for some open-faced pot roast sandwiches! I think we have some instant gravy packets too to pour on top," Harvey answered excitedly.

Captain Wilder spat into the phone, "I don't care what you make, just make sure it'll give them the energy to work all night. I'll see about taking a few minutes halfway through the pots for you to bring out some food again."

"You got it, Cap," Harvey replied.

"And Harv..." the captain whispered.

"Yes Sir?" he asked.

"Bring me one up when you get them made," Captain Wilder quietly asked him. It had been over two days since he had eaten anything other than cigarettes and coffee.

Harvey gave a quiet laugh as he acknowledged the captain's request and began working on putting together a quick meal for the crew. The preparation would normally be an easy task, except for the constant swaying of the boat back and forth which made every job twice as hard. More than once, he had lost an entire meal on the stovetop when a twenty-foot wave crashed into the boat and cleared every item off the countertops.

Today the seas were not as rough, but the ten-foot waves and thirty mile an hour gusts made it known to Harvey that they weren't on dry land. As he put the bread on the counter, the boat rolled, and the plates and jars of condiments began sliding away. During the off season, Harvey had the bright idea to install short metal bars around the countertops that prevented most of the items from falling onto the floor. However, one of the small plates slid underneath the bar and broke on the floor.

"Damn," Harvey said to himself; any time cookware broke, it came out of his paycheck. That was the deal he had made with the captain since he spent much less time out on deck. He grabbed a broom, cleaned up the shards, and dumped them into the trash can. Walking back to the counter, he began slicing the roast into thin slices before heating them up in the microwave. Once the meat was done, he put the bread down and layered the meat onto it, then loaded heaps of mash potato and finally, a thick coating of gravy.

Once a plate was made for every crewmember, including the captain, he took a second to look at the fruits of his labor. While it wouldn't be the same as having a full course meal, this would at least give the men some much needed energy to drop the last of their pots. Grabbing one of the plates, he hurried up to the wheelhouse to deliver the reward to the captain's two day fast.

******

Captain Wilder looked over his computer display that showed the layout of where he would be setting his pots. To the untrained eye, it looked like a bad 80's video game, a black screen covered in lines that marked grid squares for locations, different colored lines that marked strings of pots, and depth readings to the bottom of the ocean. His software was well outdated, he was supposed to have upgraded to the new, state-of-the-art version, but he was far away from being able to afford it after the meager fishing. While he was behind the game in terms of computers, he could read the screen like a book, knowing what every single line and symbol meant. According to the computer, they were nearing the prime spot he had set out to continue fishing.

Suddenly, the cough came back, causing him to double over the controls to his boat. Covering his mouth with his hand, he made every attempt to hold it back, but the pain was too great. Blood from his lungs spat onto the controls as tears welled up in his eyes, the pain worse than the last time. Finally, after several minutes, it subsided again.

Tom sat in his chair as he tried to catch his breath. Crossing his arms, and holding his chest, he took deep breaths to calm himself down. He could feel the pain growing in his lungs and knew that he was getting worse. The thought of how much time he had crossed his mind; he knew that after this trip he wouldn't have the strength to ride the ocean waves anymore. His head fell into his hands as he felt his entire world and way of life slipping away from him.

"Uh, you ok, boss?"

Tom turned around to see Harvey standing in the doorway holding a plate of food and staring at him with a concerned look on his face.

Reaching under the desk, Captain Wilder pulled a trash can out and spat the remaining blood into it. "I'm just great, Harvey, never better." He slid the can back underneath as he began wiping the blood off the controls.

Harvey stared at him as he looked at the desk in front of the captain and noticed the alarming amount of blood on it. With a shaky voice, he aired his concern, "Cap, I'm not one to pry into a man's business, but I think you really need to get that looked at. It's a really bad sign to be coughing up blood, especially that much."

Captain Wilder turned in his chair, his face as red as fire. He stood up and marched to Harvey, grabbing the plate from him, and throwing it against the wall, shattering it.

"You're gonna talk to me about health, you FAT FUCK?!" Captain Wilder yelled. "Look at yourself, the reason you don't ever go out on deck is because your knees can't take the strain you put on them! So, before you tell me what I should or shouldn't do with my health, how about you lose about 100 pounds and go on a diet!"

As soon as the words left his mouth, the anger left, leaving him standing there, suddenly realizing what he had just said to his crewmate. Harvey stood there, looking down at the floor, his eyes glistening, on the verge of tears. Tom couldn't believe what he had just said to him.

"I'm sorry, Captain, you're right. I'll get this cleaned up and leave you be. Sorry to upset you." Harvey spoke as if he had just found out his parents were dead. As he turned to leave the room, Tom plopped down in his chair and rubbed his temple with his aged hand.

"It's cancer, Harvey," he said quietly to the beaten down cook. "I've got cancer."

As a testament to his character, Harvey put aside the cruel words and walked to the captain's chair. "I'm so sorry, man, I had no idea."

Tom looked at Harvey. "Mike is the only one that knows,I found out before we came on this trip After this season, I'm done."

Harvey looked shocked after hearing the news. Wilder had been his Skipper for years, and now the whole boat might be out of a job.

"What about the boat, Cap? The Crew? I like working for you, and I like working on this boat," Harvey informed him.

"Don't tell this to anyone either, but Mike is gonna take over after this season is done. He's ready and he deserves it. I need to try and see if there's anything I can do to give myself some more time on this planet," Captain Wilder said as he lit a cigarette.

A look of relief washed over Harvey's face. "I agree, he's a smart guy and has been the best deck boss I could ask for. I think he'll do great."

"Good, 'cause I'm gonna have him set this string once we get to the spot so I can get some sleep," Tom informed him.

"That sounds like a good idea. Well, I'm gonna get this mess cleaned up and head back down. I'm sorry again about the bad news," Harvey expressed with sympathy.

As he turned to leave, the captain spoke, "I didn't mean what I said, Harvey. I don't know why I said those things, you're one of the best guys I have had work under me and you sure as hell don't ever complain. But, I'm sorry, you're a good man."

Finally, it was Harvey's turn to say something the other didn't want to hear. "I know exactly why you said it, you found out you have cancer, boss. I don't blame you for being upset. Believe me, I've looked this way for a long time, I can take some harsh words. But, thank you. I don't want our last season together to end in yells and screams."

Harvey stuck out his hand, which the captain took, and gave a firm handshake.

CHAPTER SIX:

In the galley, Mike finished his meal, sitting next to his fellow crewmates while they all let the food digest before their long shift began. He leaned back and allowed his eyes to close before the galley phone began ringing. Harvey walked over and picked the phone up to answer it.

"Hello," Harvey spoke into the receiver. "Yeah, you got it, boss,"

Harvey hung the phone up and turned towards Mike. "Captain wants to see you up in the wheelhouse, man."

"For fucks sake," Mike grunted as he pulled himself up from the table. The only thing he wanted right now was to shut his eyes for a few minutes before another long day. Instead, he was walking up the stairs, most likely to perform another mundane task before they got started. Opening the door, he walked into the captain's office, and stood behind him before letting him know that he was there. "You wanted to see me, Cap?" Mike asked.

Captain Wilder stood up from his chair and stretched, turning to Mike. "Yeah, I did, I want you to set this string of pots, Mike. I need to get some sleep and I figured you could use the practice since you're gonna be doing this full time soon."

Mike stood in shock, not expecting the news he had just been given. "Wow, yeah, absolutely, Tom. Thank you."

"No, thank you. I haven't slept in days, and I need some rest. Just keep her as straight as possible while you're setting and go at a steady pace. Don't let the guys set the tone, you need to set it. They're gonna start complaining and slowing down once they start getting cold and wet, keep on them. After all the years working out there, you know when it's too dangerous to work and when they're just being a bunch of pussies. And don't take any shit from them, especially Justin."

Mike nodded and walked to the chair and sat down, letting the reality finally sink in. This would be the first time that he was not going to be on deck to help the rest of the crew. Instead, he was the one in charge of setting ninety pots and making sure no one got hurt. The other times he had sat up here was on watch, and a couple of times he was even able to set only a couple of pots. But now, a large part of their season was going to be riding on his shoulders.

Tom walked behind Mike and put his hand on his shoulder. "You're gonna do just fine, Mike. Trust your gut, and don't get upset if you don't land right on them. This job is all about fine tuning how you set the strings after you see what you pull up. If something serious happens, wake me up."

"Thank you, Tom, I'll find 'em," Mike replied.

Tom laughed as he walked out the door. "I know you will, brother, just make sure to save some crab for me to catch."

******

The squid swam in a frenzy, its food source was gone. The crab had disappeared and were nowhere to be seen. It had been days since the monster of the deep had had anything to eat, and it was growing incredibly malicious from the hunger it felt. Swimming tens of miles, it scoured every inch of the ocean floor looking for any sign of food. The cold of the water constricted its body as the tentacles raced behind the massive head, the urge to feed growing more maddening by the second.

All of a sudden, the squid spotted an object on the ocean bed, and dove at it with more aggression than the ocean had ever seen. It lunged with its tentacles, scooping the creature into its beak and began biting and ripping it apart. Quickly, it realized it was not prey, but one of the devises used to hold the crustations that it chose to feed on. Spitting the pieces of metal from its beak, it grabbed onto one of them and brought it to its enormous eye.

This one appeared different, the other ones it had encountered before were decayed and incredibly old, this one appeared shiny and even had a couple of fish in it that it quickly grabbed and ate. Looking along the seabed, off in the distance was the outline of another trap; something was putting these things here and taking away its food source. Racing to it, the creature could smell that the trap had a fresh smell of fish, meaning whatever had put it here couldn't be far away. It looked across from where the last two traps were and saw another. It quickly concluded that if it followed the path of the traps, it would find the creature that was starving it to death.

Darting with newfound energy, the monster raced in the direction of the next trap, stopping to destroy it and eat the pungent fish inside, and continued to the next one. With each metal trap it discovered, the anger inside of it grew; something in this ocean dared challenge it. Not only challenge it but try and kill it without direct combat. This meant that this new creature was afraid of it, which brought the closest feeling of joy the squid was able to feel. The mind of the squid started to plunge into curiosity as it raced faster, contemplating how big this enemy must be and how much nourishment it would bring to its stomach.

******

The need for sleep grew on Mike as he continued pushing the crew harder than he ever imagined he could. He had lost track of what time it was, but the sky outside had turned pitch black as the wind grew to gusts of over forty miles an hour. Out on deck, the men were beginning to reach their breaking point, mistakes began occurring more often and tempers were flaring up. More than once, Mike could hear the quiet voices of the crew questioning how come he wasn't out there with the rest of them, leaving the deck a man short.

While Mike was able to keep the men doing their jobs, he realized how much more there was to being the captain of a crab boat. His words were the final decision for not just the crew, but for the equipment as well. With every pot that he set, he grew more unsure if he was setting in the right spot; the worst part being he wouldn't know until the pots soaked and they pulled them up.

To add to his already challenging task, the deck was growing slick from the snow and freezing ocean water that covered the wooden boards and metal. He stared into the camera monitor to keep an eye on the crew; the picture was very fuzzy, and he was only able to tell who was who by their jackets. This camera system was long overdue for an upgrade, just like so many other things on the boat. The only thing he could do was watch out for the men as best as he could, and always keep an account on where everyone was.

******

On deck, the men were exhausted and becoming sloppy in their work. While Mike was up in the wheelhouse, John oversaw the deck and made sure everyone was performing their jobs. His nerves were growing thin from Justin, who hadn't stop complaining since they began dropping pots. More than once, he had to tell Justin to shut up and do his job. With over forty-five pots left before this string was done, there were plenty of hours left before they were able to call it a day.

The air was cold, wind blowing at well over forty miles an hour, and the waves were climbing over the rails on occasion. The boat rocked back and forth as the engines powered through the seas, straining when it had to overcome the bigger waves. Laying pots in calm seas was a labor inducing challenge, but during the night with seas such as this, any mistake could prove to be fatal.

John worked the hydraulic crane and set the next pot down onto the launcher while Travis and Mitchell secured it and opened it up. Kyle came running with the bait and hopped in, securing it inside the pot and jumped out while the two closed and secured the door. From the wheelhouse, Mike hit the horn and gave the signal to launch.

Just as the horn sounded, chaos erupted on deck. Justin's job at the moment was to unlatch the next pot from the rest of the stack so it could be picked up by the crane. As soon as he loosened the chain, the boat was hit by a twenty-foot wave across the side, and the pot began sliding across the deck. Eight hundred pounds of solid steel slid back and forth as the boat pitched. Mike, trying to keep control of the boat, yelled on the intercom for the men to get out of its way.

Kyle and Justin jumped out of the way just in time as the pot came racing towards them and they scurried to the corner of the bait station, the pot slamming into the side of the railing.

Mitchell stood in shock, then raced to the hydraulic station where John was and jumped on top of him, protected by the controls welded to the decking. Travis, being a muscular man, stood at the railing where he was, waiting for his chance to try and stop the pot once it came to a rest and get it resecured.

******

In the wheelhouse, Mike was in a panic. He tried to keep the boat straight as he watched the carnage ensue. So far, the runaway pot had almost killed two crewmembers, and was bouncing between the rails like a pinball machine. Checking to get an account of everyone, he spotted Travis, and could tell what he was about to do.

"Travis!! Just stay clear of the pot! Don't try and grab onto it!" Mike yelled into the microphone.

A warning light flashed to life on the control panel in front of him, taking his attention off the deck. The light was for the engine pressure. He checked the gauge and watched the needle slowly creep to the right, meaning their pressure was building to the point they might blow one of the engines. He turned and grabbed the phone across from him and called Captain Wilder, leaving his back turned from the window overlooking the deck.

******

Travis saw his opportunity; the boat was leveling, and the pot was about to come to a stop. If he was fast enough, he could secure a line to it and keep it contained in one area long enough to use the crane to pick it up. He looked around and couldn't see anyone else, meaning this would all be on him. At least he would have Mike watching over him, and see he wasn't afraid of a hunk of mindless metal. The boat became level, and the pot came to a stop, this was his chance. He ran forward as fast as he could, turning on his flashlight clipped to his jacket to help him see. But he was suddenly stopped by immense pressure around his waist that sucked all the air out of him and stopped him in his tracks. Confused, he looked down and saw a thick red tentacle wrapped around him, constricting tighter and making him gasp.

Travis tried to move his feet forward as he felt it pull him back towards the rail, where he saw this "thing" seemed to continue over into the ocean. Looking up towards the wheelhouse, Travis tried to scream for Mike, or for anyone to help, and felt himself being squeezed so tight, he felt like his guts were going to shoot out of his mouth.

No matter how hard he tried, he was helpless as he was pulled over the railing, and felt the freezing water surround him. He thrashed his arms around in the pitch-black water, looking around, trying to find the source of what was holding onto him. His flashlight caught brief glimpses of numerous red tentacles swaying around him, before he felt the one holding onto him pulling him further away from the boat. He was being held by some kind of monster, and it wanted his flesh.

Travis' mind raced, scared, and confused about what was happening, and what was going to happen to him. One thing he knew for sure though, with water this cold, he would be dead in another minute, easing his worries about having to experience the pain of being eaten alive.

Before he was able to drift into unconsciousness, he felt extreme pain in his back, like a mad man had scooped out a part of his back with a shovel. Travis screamed with every ounce of air he had left in his lungs, never imagining the ability to feel pain as horrible as this. The pain sent a shockwave through his body, sending adrenaline coursing through his veins, and keeping him fully alert to what was happening to him.

Another scoop was taken out of his back, the water in front of his flashlight turning dark red. All Travis wanted now was just to die, for this rollercoaster of pain to finally end and let him answer for the deeds of his life. Before he could get his wish, all his arms and legs fully extended, each held by a thick red tentacle at the ends. With great force, Travis felt his arms and legs being pulled apart from his body.

He felt every muscle strand slowly being pulled from each other, all his pain spent in the gym was now adding to the pain he felt now. The bones in his arms were snapped in half as the tentacles holding them made a whipping motion, the skin tearing apart finally as Travis' arms disappeared from his view and his body.

Finally succumbing to the extreme blood loss, Travis could feel his wish for death was seconds away from being granted. His eyelids closing, his head rolled forward, giving him his last view of life. He watched as the three-foot beak of the monster rose up and bit into him, cutting him nearly in half.

******

The squid finished devouring this new creature. Whilst it took more work than the crab to get to, the meat was delicious. Already, it could feel the energy coming back to its body and bringing the warmth back. While the tentacle was grabbing the creature from its home above the water, it could sense through tiny spine-like hairs on the appendage that there were other creatures living in the same location.

Now, the squid would continue to follow this large enemy, and devour all the organisms that dared protect it.

CHAPTER SEVEN:

Captain Wilder heard the phone in his captain's quarters ringing. He rolled over and picked it up.

"Yeah. What's up, Mike?" he asked.

Mike's voice pounded through the phone, "I need you up here now, Tom!! Everything's going to hell right now!"

Tom sat up in his bed. "Woah, slow down, Mike. What's going on?"

"One of the engines is overheating, we have a pot that got away and is sliding around the deck, and... Wait... where's Travis?" Mike asked in a panic.

Tom's heart sank to the bottom of his stomach, the words turning his blood ice cold.

"He should be on the deck with the rest of the guys..." Wilder addressed the panicked deck boss.

"Holy shit, get up here! I think we have a man overboard!"

******

Tom ran up the stairs to the wheelhouse and yanked the door open, letting it slam behind him as he saw Mike, a look of panic streaked across his face.

"We can't find him, Tom..." Mike said as he pulled his hair with his fingers.

Captain Wilder looked at him in shock and confusion. "What do you mean we can't find him?"

"I mean he's gone," Mike replied gravely. "Kyle and Mitchell got the pot secured and the rest of the guys have checked every inch of the deck, Travis is gone. They have the search lights on and there's no sign of him in the water either."

"Were you guys setting pots when that one got loose?" Captain Wilder asked him.

"Yeah, right when that pot came undone, Travis was launching one over the side."

"Oh shit," Tom muttered as he ran his hand through his hair. "He must have gotten his foot caught in the line as the pot got launched and it pulled him over."

Mike looked at him for a second before questioning him, "That couldn't have happened though, Tom, I swear I saw him standing there after the pot was over the side already. He was going to try and grab the loose pot right before I called you, and when I turned back, he was gone."

"There's a lot of line attached to those things, we're dropping deep. There's plenty of time for him to get caught up even if he thought he was in the clear. Anyways, the seas aren't bad enough to have made him fall overboard, it had to have been the buoy line," Captain Wilder reasoned.

Something didn't feel right to Mike, he was sure the buoys were already off the boat before Travis went to grab the pot. Travis was one of the most experienced guys on deck, he would have known to keep clear of the line when they were launching. But there was one thing Mike knew for sure, he was gone.

"I'll take over the wheelhouse, you go out on deck and help get the rest of those pots set, Mike," Tom ordered.

"What about Travis?" Mike asked gravely.

"He's gone," Captain Wilder spoke with a cold tone. "By now he's at the bottom of the ocean. With the water as cold as it is, he at least had a quick death."

******

Out on deck, hardly a word was spoken amongst the crew while the rest of the pots were set into the sea. None of them would look at Mike, some because they couldn't imagine what was going through his mind after what had happened, and others because they blamed him for the death of their friend. Justin kept his head down during his work, but at moments would look up and glare at him.

"His death is on your hands, you piece of shit," Justin muttered to himself as he untied the last pot on the deck.

"I'd watch what you say and who you say it around, Justin."

Startled, Justin turned around and saw John standing over him, glaring into his soul. He leaned down to match Justin's crouched stance and brought his face inches away from him.

"If I ever hear you talk about Mike like that again, I'll beat you within an inch of your life, you understand me?" John said coldly. "What happened was an accident, it wasn't anyone's fault, especially Mike's. Once your foot's in that line, you have seconds, that's it. Even if Mike had seen it, none of us would have been able to get to him in time."

Justin couldn't shake the feeling of resentment towards the deck boss. "He should have done something though, man. And he comes out on deck and acts like nothing happened, like we're all just supposed to be ok with one of our guys dying on his watch."

The boat rocked, causing Justin to slip and fall on his back. John let a smile grow across his face as he extended a hand to help him up, savoring the justice from the sea.

"Imagine what's going through his mind right now, man," John said as he helped him back onto his feet. "Imagine having something like this happen on your first time at the helm, and then having to go out and keep doing your job. Trying to keep your attention on the work while the thought of losing someone races through your head. That is more punishment than I would ever wish on another man. Think about that."

John turned to walk away and heard Justin take another jab at Mike.

"Still doesn't change the fact that we're now a man short to do all the work and no extra pay with it."

The ship's engineer turned and kicked Justin as hard as he could in the leg, sending him collapsing to the ground before jumping on top of him. John grabbed him by the front of his jacket and punched him straight in the nose. Blinded by rage, he kept hitting him until he felt multiple pairs of hands pull him off.

Overhead, the loudspeaker began booming throughout the boat. "What the hell is going on down there?? Break it up!! Get those two apart NOW!!" the captain yelled.

Mike grabbed his friend and pulled him away from the pummeled man lying on the ground. "What the hell is going on, John!? You know the rules, no fighting! What's the matter with you?"

John shrugged Mike's hands off of him and started walking away to try and cool down. He pulled a cigarette from his jacket and lit it as he continued walking in circles, his heart beating through his chest from anger.

"He wouldn't keep his damn mouth shut, that's what's the matter with me!" John yelled as he looked to see Kyle and Mitchell dragging Justin back to the crew quarters.

"Dude, you can't just hit him because he runs his mouth! Look at him, you knocked him out. This is the last thing we need right now after everything that's happened today." Mike stopped before lowering his voice, "Now we're short two men on deck, man."

The words stung Mike as soon as they left his mouth, bringing the realization back to him of their lost crew member.

John slowly walked towards him. "That's why I hit him, man, he's been saying nothing but horrible shit about you. Blaming you for what happened. I told him to stop, and he kept going. Finally, I had enough."

John threw his cigarette over the rail without finishing it. "What happened wasn't your fault, Mike, and I'm not gonna let anyone say it was. It was an accident, and there was nothing you could have done to stop it."

Going straight to the deck after the incident, Mike hadn't had much time to reflect on what had happened and process everything. He sat down on an overturned bucket and put his hands over his mouth, thinking of how the captain of a boat would handle what was happening to the crew.

"I appreciate you sticking up for me, but Justin has a reason to be upset. One of his friends just died, and even if you don't think it was directly my fault, if I had been watching him, we might have been able to cut the line before he went over," Mike said grimly.

John crouched down. "You can't blame yourself for everything that happens, Mike. Sometimes bad shit just happens. You did the right thing by calling for Wilder to come up, and you made sure the engine didn't blow, which would have put us in an even bigger world of shit. I'll still follow you on this boat, man, nothing about what happened today is gonna change that."

"Can I ask you a question?" Mike asked him.

"Shoot."

Mike had a complex look on his face as he thought about how to word what he wanted to say. "Do you think Travis got his foot caught in the pot line?"

John looked confused. "What do you mean?"

"I mean, when I last saw him, I'm almost one hundred percent sure that line was gone before he went over the side. Something just doesn't add up."

"I don't know, it seemed to me that was the only thing that could have happened. No one pushed him over, and the ocean sure as hell didn't pull him in. Did you check the deck camera?"

"No, I haven't," Mike answered. "With how old that system is, I doubt I would be able to see anything. It'd just be a waste of time." He had a hard look of defeat on his face as he stared down at the deck.

John tried throwing him a bone to help put him at ease. "What's the harm in checking it at least? One of the cameras should be looking right at the railing where Travis was standing, and it would be in full view of the line from the pot. As shitty as this is to say, I think if you see him get caught in it, it'll help put your mind at ease. You'll know what happened and that will help your mind to stop racing about other possibilities."

Standing up, Mike knew that John was right, and as hard as it was going to be to watch his friend die on the video, it was the only way for him to come to terms with what had happened.

"I think you're right, thank you, John." Mike gave him a hug, a gesture of affection that is rarely seen on any boat, even for a crew that had been together for many years.

"I don't want to see you do anything drastic or crazy because your mind is racing," John explained. "I've seen guys that couldn't handle seeing their friends die, and they went and offed themselves. I don't want to see that happen to you."

"I don't think you'll have to worry about that, man," Mike chuckled. "I can't leave this deck any more shorthanded than it already is."

"Are you two SHITBAGS done with your grab assing?!?!" Captain Wilder screamed again over the intercom. "Mike, tell that engineer to get his ass up here NOW!! His ass is in deep shit!"

Walking to the ready room, both men knew that the conversation with John and the captain was going to be very heated. Fighting on a boat was not tolerated at all, not to mention knocking the man out.

Captain Wilder wasn't done though with berating the engineer over the loud speaker. "Hurry up, John!! We can't finish this string until after I'm done with you up here! Everyone tell John thank you for making you work longer because he decided to knock out one of the other dumbasses on the boat."

A quiet smile grew across John's face; he knew that if the captain was talking how he was, he would have most of his steam blown off by the time he got to the wheelhouse. Maybe enough to where he would keep his job.

"Hey Mike, get that greenhorn to clean the blood off the deck, the last thing we need is for anyone else to get whatever he has from those women he visits," Captain Wilder yelled.

******

Kyle grabbed one of the empty buckets off the deck and took it to the kitchen. Filling it up and adding some bleach, he grabbed a scrub brush and went back outside where he found a sizable amount of blood leftover from the one-sided fight. Apparently, Justin was a bleeder when it came to injuries, he thought to himself. He got on his knees and began scrubbing the deck, allowing time for the bleach to kill anything that might have been in Justin's blood.

Once the deck was cleaned, Kyle picked up the bucket with the rest of the water and splashed it over the cleaned surface. He watched the red-tinted water race into the slot at the base of the deck where the water ran off into the ocean. Satisfied that the crew could now eat off of that spot, he returned the bucket to the ready room, and prepared to spend another untold number of hours finishing their last string.

******

Under the water's surface, the eye of the giant squid observed blood coming from the large creature. Its senses went into a whirlwind when it caught the scent of the blood, confirming its instinct to stalk and hunt this new prey. A creature of this size would not be easy to kill, it would have to use every tool in its arsenal to bring it down. But the instinctual urge to rip it in half and enjoy what lay inside was too great for the squid to resist. It would now begin the process of killing it, letting patience and persistence work to its advantage.

******

The rest of the shift was a grind from hell for the crew, the only saving grace was Harvey coming out on deck to help finish up the string. It took another five hours to get the rest of the pots in the water, and by the end of it, the crew had become robots. Every action had become automatic, energy couldn't be spent on thinking about what they were going to do next. When the last pot had dropped, the crew stumbled to the ready room and began stripping out of their work gear. Five men wearing Long Johns walked to their rooms to get some much needed sleep.

Just before Mike opened the door to his room, he remembered what John had said about the camera overlooking the deck. He turned and headed to the wheelhouse to pull the memory card from the camera system.

When he got to the door of the wheelhouse, Mike stopped for a moment before knocking, considering what the captain would say when he asked to look at the footage.

"Come in," Wilder's voice rang from inside.

Mike turned the doorknob and walked into the dimly lit room, the only light coming from the glow of the instrument panel.

Captain Wilder looked at him and shook his head. "I'm surprised you're not asleep right now, Mike, too tired?"

He chuckled, "Not exactly, boss. I was wondering if I could get the memory card for the deck camera and look at some footage for a minute. If that's ok with you."

"Knock yourself out, Mike. Take all the time you need with it. Just promise me one thing though while you're looking at it." Captain Wilder turned the whole chair to face his longtime friend.

"What's that?" Mike asked.

"Get some closure and put this behind you. Being a captain, this is a reality of the job that we do. I hope you never have to experience anything like what happened today again, but this is one of the hazards of the job. Travis knew that. One of the hardest parts about working on a boat is you can do everything right and sometimes the worst still happens. You accept that, and you'll be ok," Captain Wilder reasoned with him.

Mike nodded and gave his reassurance that he would and walked out to go back to his room.

******

Mike opened the door to his quarters and let it close behind him, the day finally catching up to him as he collapsed into his bed. He rolled over and pulled his duffle bag out from under the bed frame and took out his laptop. Setting it on his lap, he inserted the memory sim card into the slot on his computer and opened the app to begin reviewing the footage.

He fast forwarded to the point where the pot began racing around the deck, going frame by frame to be sure he didn't miss any details. With each frame, he felt his eyelids droop more and more, sleep about to overtake him.

Suddenly, something caught Mike's attention that made his eyes shoot open and made him fully alert. As he continued frame by frame, he spotted Travis on the deck, trying to grab onto the pot, but there was something that was stopping him. Mike squinted to try and make out what it was, the grainy picture making it a harder task than it needed to be.

Finally, after a couple more frames, he could make out what appeared to be a thick red rope hugging Travis' waist. Looking next to where he stood, Mike noticed that the pot and buoy lines were already off the deck. This meant Travis never got pulled over because of the pot being launched.

Instead of putting his mind to rest though, more questions started racing through his mind, one being what was that thing attached to Travis' waist? They didn't have any line that was red in color on the boat, and it appeared that it originated from the other side of the railing, the ocean. Letting the video play at normal speed now, Mike could see Travis was struggling to move forward, and noticed he was being pulled towards the railing.

After watching for about another minute, Travis was finally taken over the side. Mike rewatched the footage three times, making sure he wasn't just seeing what he wanted to see. He realized that something strange was going on, his friend wasn't killed because of some kind of accident. While he didn't know what was going on, he made a promise to his deceased friend that he would learn the truth.

Looking at his watch, Mike realized he had been up looking at the video for over an hour, exhaustion and fatigue had finally settled in. He made the decision to show the captain in the morning what he had found and to get some rest.

Before he put his computer away, Mike looked at the screen one last time, staring at the strange red thing attached to his friend and tapped the screen.

"What are you?"

CHAPTER EIGHT:

Mike woke after four hours, not as much sleep as he would have liked, but enough for him to function for the day. He walked out of his room just as John was leaving his, both giving a nod to each other as they walked toward the coffee pot and filled a mug. Sitting down at the galley table, they rubbed the sleep out of their eyes and waited for breakfast to be served. Harvey, at his usual station in the kitchen, was making spam and scrambled eggs for breakfast.

John was the first to break the silence as he leaned in towards Mike. "Did you get a chance to look at the camera footage before you clocked out?"

Mike looked at him and debated what exactly to tell him, not even fully knowing what he had seen on the video.

"I saw something really weird, John," Mike whispered. "Travis didn't get pulled by the pot that was in the launcher, he went over well after the buoy lines were already over the rail."

"What the hell happened to him then?" John asked. "Did he slip over or something?"

"I'm not exactly sure, but in the video, I could see some kind of red rope that was wrapped around his waist before he went over the side," Mike informed him.

John gave him a confused look. "What do you mean a red rope? We don't have any rope that's that color."

"I know, that's what's confusing me. And it doesn't make sense because it wraps around him from over the side, coming from the ocean," Mike said.

"That's really fucking weird, man. Have you told the captain yet?" John asked.

Mike looked down again. "No, not yet. I don't know what to say to him. The only thing I know for sure is it wasn't the buoy line that pulled Travis overboard."

"Maybe we snagged a line from another boat's pot and have been pulling it with us for a while; how it would have come over the rail, I have no idea," John reasoned.

His mind tried to think of any logical reason to explain what happened, but nothing made sense to Mike. "I guess that's a possibility, hell, I don't know. This is getting more unusual by the minute. I'm gonna take a look where Travis went over once we get out on deck, maybe there will be something there to kinda explain things."

John nodded as he agreed with the idea. "Smart thinking, maybe a piece of the rope will be there with some clue to where it came from."

"I hope so," Mike replied.

Just then, Harvey walked over with plates for the two men, steam rising from them as he set them down on the table. Harvey had a gloomy look on his face instead of his usual cheerful expression.

"Sad news about Travis, fellas," he said somberly. "He was a damn good man and a great crewman. Aways enjoyed my cooking too." He looked down at the floor and tried to think of something more meaningful to say about him but failed. "Try and enjoy the food, guys."

Mike gave Harvey a nod as he walked back to the kitchen. "Thanks, Harv."

He looked over at the counter and noticed there was one plate too many; Harvey had made a plate for Travis. A lump formed in his throat as Harvey looked to see what Mike was staring at.

"Oh, I'm sorry, man, force of habit." Harvey went over to throw the extra plate of food away, dumping it in the trash can.

"It's gonna take a lot of getting used to for all of us not having him around anymore," Mike said in a low voice, the words stinging as his emotions began hitting him again with the loss of his friend.

John hadn't said anything, barely touching his food; Travis' death had hit him the hardest. Even though he wouldn't let the others see it, John was devastated once reality set in that he would never see one of his best friends again. Many times, they would go to the local bar together and spend the night drinking and getting into trouble. Those days were now gone.

"I'm gonna get ready to start hauling pots. I'll be throwing the hook if you don't have any objections, Mike," John said as he stood up to leave.

"No, go right ahead, man. You're the best hook thrower on the boat now," Mike answered.

Sitting at the table alone now, Mike thought to himself when would be the best time to tell the captain about what he had seen on the video. Now wasn't the right time, he decided, emotions were still too high. Hopefully they would have a great haul from their pots, and then he would bring up his discovery.

He finished his breakfast and got dressed for the long day ahead of them. While the rest of the crew ate, Mike walked out onto the deck; there was something he had to check before they started work.

******

Mike inspected the deck and the railing and couldn't find a single clue to what really happened to his friend. His mind tried to think of anywhere else he could look to give him some answers but drew a blank. Spotting a bucket lying on its side, he kicked it as hard as he could, sending it flying, almost hitting Kyle.

"Oh shit," Kyle yelled as he narrowly dodged it.

"What are you doing out here, Kyle, shouldn't you be getting ready for the shift?" Mike asked him.

"I came out here to have a few minutes to think before we started. I didn't know you were doing the same thing, Mike, I'll leave you be." Kyle started to walk away before Mike stopped him.

"Did you see anything unusual out here last night before you went in?" Mike asked him.

Kyle thought for a moment. "No, not that I can... well, there was something that I thought was weird."

Mike raised an eyebrow. "What is it?"

"Well, there was some kind of weird slime stuff on the deck by the rail, I don't know where it came from. But I noticed it after I cleaned up the blood from Justin. I took a walk to clear my head and stepped in a little pool of it," Kyle informed him.

Slime, what the hell could that have come from? Mike thought to himself.

"You sure it wasn't hydraulic fluid from the crane?" Mike asked.

"Positive, man, this stuff was really thick, and smelled like rotten meat. I had to scoop it up with a dust pan just to get it off."

Mike stood there, more confused than ever. "Where did you find it?"

Kyle pointed towards the railing, at the same spot that Travis went overboard.

"You're sure that's where you found it, Kyle?" Mike asked, getting tunnel vision as he looked at the railing.

"Yeah, it was right next to the pot launcher, which I thought was weird. At first, I thought it came from the launcher, but I checked the whole thing, nothing's leaking from it. And that's the only spot I found it in."

Things just got more bizarre by the minute on this boat.

"Ok, thanks, man. Why don't you go get ready, I'll let the captain know about it." Mike started to walk to the wheelhouse intercom.

Kyle stopped him with the one question that Mike didn't have an answer to. "What the hell's going on, Mike?"

"I don't know, Kyle," Mike answered him.

He walked away and began heading to the ready room but quickly stopped in his tracks. Mike looked at the ground and noticed some pieces of meat lying on the deck. Very quickly he realized the meat belonged to the whole cod fish that they kept for the crab pots. The meat formed a trail that went from the white tote that they were kept in and continued to the railing. Mike studied the trail, confused at why the fish were torn apart and not where they were stored.

"What the hell is going on?" he asked himself. None of the crew would have done this, there was no reason to. Tearing apart the cod would only have meant doing extra work, which none of the men would ever consider doing. And why was the fish leading to the side of the boat?

Mike walked over to the bait station and yelled into the speaker, "Hey Cap, there's some really weird shit going on here. I think it may be serious."

The captain returned Mike's concern with his usual response, "It can wait till later, Mike, we got our first string coming up in a couple of miles. Get back inside and make sure the guys are all ready to start. Everything else can wait, we got fishing to do."

Mike hung his head and debated telling him anyway about what he had seen this morning. Adding everything up, his curiosity was quickly turning into concern, not just for the boat, but for the safety of the crew. First Travis was pulled overboard by something that came out of the sea, then the strange mucus around the railing, and now a fish that looked like something was having a go at it and liked it. But orders were orders, the captain was in charge and what he says goes.

Mike took one last look at the ocean before heading inside. For some reason, he couldn't help but think that all of the strange things he had seen these last couple of days were all connected to each other. He closed the door behind him and saw the rest of the crew putting their waterproof coveralls on. Walking to the coat rack, he found his pair and put them on.

"You all ready for a good haul today?" Mike asked them, trying to bring their spirits up.

Justin sneered at him, "Oh yeah, we're gonna just hit the motherlode today, man. In fact, we're gonna get so many crab in this first string we can all just go home."

John shoved Justin from behind. "No one fucking asked you, man. Keep your opinions to yourself if you're just gonna be a negative Nancy."

Justin quickly spun around to face John. "You think you're so tough 'cause you sucker punched me, don't ya?" Now it was Justin's turn to do the pushing, as he threw his hands out at John, causing him to stumble back.

Mike ran in between the two and grabbed each by their collars. "Hey, that's enough!! You're lucky the captain didn't fire both of you last night; you can bet your asses you do it again and you won't be so lucky!"

Both men glared at each other as Mike pushed them both away. "We still have a whole trip's worth of fishing left to do so knock it off! This isn't the way to start our first set of hauling. Stay away from each other and don't say anything unless it's related to bringing a pot on board. This is the last time I'm gonna say anything about it. One more fight and I'll have the captain turn the boat around and head back to port. Am I clear?"

Both men gave a nod as they did their best to cool off before walking out onto the deck. Tensions were high for everyone as the lack of sleep and the events from the night before began to take their toll. Mike knew he would have to be on his game today and keep the men focused on what was important, fishing. They couldn't afford any more accidents being they were already a man short for the rest of the trip.

Captain Wilder's voice boomed from the speakers, "We got the first buoy coming up! Everyone get ready and let's kick this thing in the ass!!"

John ran to his spot at the rail and grabbed the hook from its holder; aside from Travis, he was the next best thrower. The rest of the crew got to their spots, Mike at the hydraulic controls, Justin and Mitchell on standby to grab the pot once it came over the rail, and Kyle at his bait station, ready to rebait the pot if it held a large number of crab.

Within minutes, John could see the two bright orange buoys floating in the water. Once the boat was several feet from them, he threw the hook with all of his strength. The men watched as the grappling hook flew through the air with the rope that was attached trailing behind it. It landed perfectly in between both buoys and hooked onto the line connected to the pot.

John grabbed the line and began pulling it hand over hand as fast as he could. Once the first buoy was in the boat, he set the rope into the crab block. Mike activated the controls and watched the block reel in the line, pulling the pot up from the depths. Everyone watched in anticipation, waiting for the pot to break the surface and reveal if they had set in the right spot. Captain Wilder chewed his fingernails as the top of the pot broke the surface.

Grabbing the hook attached to the crane, John hooked it to the two part line connected to the top of the large, rectangular pot and gave Mike a thumbs up. Operating the crane, Mike maneuvered the control levers and hoisted the pot above the water's surface.

All the men on deck cheered the loudest they ever had before, staring in amazement at the pot that was filled at the top with hundreds of live Opilio crab. They had set in the right spot. Captain Wilder threw his hat in the air as he cheered along with the crew, believing his run of bad luck had finally turned around.

As the pot cleared the water, Justin and Mitchell each grabbed a side and turned it around and set it into the launcher. Mike activated the controls to the dogs and secured the pot in place. Hundreds of crab legs were sticking outside the lacings of the pot as they tried to escape their fate. John walked to the sorting table that was kept off to the side and wheeled it over to the bottom of the pot and opened the lid.

The crab fell out like an avalanche, covering the whole table with one-pound crustations. The deckhands quickly ran to the table to begin the process of sorting all of the crab, throwing any females back into the ocean and any ones too small to keep. Harvey came out from the galley and aided in the sorting process. Mike even called the greenhorn over because all hands were needed to do this quickly and accurately.

"How do I know which ones are keepers?" Kyle asked as he inspected the crab and made every effort not to get his fingers pinched.

Mike again realized how new Kyle was to the fishing game, wishing even more to have Travis back on the deck. "Turn them upside down and look at the abdomen. If it's circular, it's a female and we need to get rid of it. If its pointed, it's a male. Use that measuring tool on the table and make sure they're big enough to keep. And don't forget to keep a count of how many keepers you got as you dump them in the tank. I need a count to give to the captain."

Kyle sorted as fast as he could but was falling behind compared to the rest of the crew. He noticed he was the only one needing to use the measuring tool as the others could tell just by looking at them if they were big enough to keep. He looked over at Harvey and watched him grabbing large handfuls of crab and stuffing them into the holding tank below.

John saw Kyle staring at the ship's cook and laughed. "It's ok if you're impressed, man, Harvey's the best crab sorter in the fleet. He has got a special gift for picking out bad crab in a pile. It must be because he cooks with them so much!"

Harvey gave him a rounded smile as he scooped up another pile of crab and put them into the tank. "What can I say, man. If it has to do with some kind of food, I'm the best at it."

The rest of the crew gave a laugh as they finished sorting. After five minutes and a few pinched fingers, the table was finally cleared. Mike got the numbers from all the deckhands and was more than pleased with the number he would be giving to the captain.

Walking back to the speaker, Mike yelled, "Seven-hundred-and-twenty, Seven-Two-Zero!!"

Once again, the crew cheered as the captain yelled back, "That's what I'm talking about, guys!! We haven't seen numbers like that in years!! If we can keep numbers like this up, we'll be heading back to offload in no time!"

After the celebration was done, they went back to their positions on deck and prepared for the next pot. John threw the hook and landed it perfectly again. As the pot came above the water, they saw that this one was also almost filled to the top with crab. Over the next fifteen hours, the men watched as pot after pot came over the side and brought forth the bounty of the Bering Sea. Consistent numbers of 600 to 800 crab per pot were the reward for all of their hard work, the best fishing any of them had seen in a long time.

Finally, the last pot was hauled and sorted, yielding a crab count of 900 to finish off the string. Captain Wilder made the decision to load the pots onto the deck instead of setting them back, waiting to see how their second string fared to see if he should dump every pot he had in this area.

The crew was tired, but still riding on the high of amazing fishing. John took the first watch at the wheel, letting the captain and the rest of the crew get some needed rest as the boat headed to their second string. Harvey was in the galley preparing a quick snack for all of them before they turned in to their bunks. The crew munched on some sandwiches and chips which they washed down with several bottles of Gatorade. Once their stomachs were satisfied, the crew shuffled to their bunks and quickly fell asleep.

******

John sat in the wheelhouse and watched the course heading on the GPS screen as the boat continued its journey. He looked over at the pressure gauge for the engines and noticed the left engine was struggling again. The dial slowly climbed higher and higher, worrying the engineer. Deciding to go down to the engine room, he took a flashlight and left the boat on autopilot, walking out of the room to see if there was anything to be done for the struggling engine.

******

Just as the door was closed, a tentacle slithered across the deck and raced to the hold where the crabs were stored. Using the massive suction cups on the end, it opened the lid. Snaking the tentacle into the opening, it could sense thousands of moving crab inside, realizing they were completely trapped. The squid closed its arm around a cluster and brought it back over the rail, taking it directly to the awaiting beak.

Armload after armload of crabs were taken from the boat, feeding the large beast of the sea. Gaining the energy it had lost following the large, slow-moving creature, it would now be able to continue to stalk and give it time to plan an attack that would kill it.

After it had emptied the storage container of every last crab, the squid finally retracted the long tentacle back to its body and swam away, keeping the strange creature in the visual of its eye.

Distance was going to be crucial until the time was right, when the squid would make the move to kill instead of scavenging off the beast. Patience was an art, and this creature was the master of it.

******

In the engine room, John did everything he could think of to give the struggling engine an ounce more of life. He added more oil and checked for any leaks or broken parts. After finding none, he knew the engine was simply old and had been through too much. He estimated they would lose it any day and they would have to turn back to port for a new one. With how well the fishing had been today, that was going to be a very painful trip back. Luckily, the boat used two engines, but going down to one was going to eat up a large amount of time just trying to get back. Making his way back to the wheelhouse, he sat back in the chair to resume the rest of his watch. He glanced at the speedometer on the dash and noticed the boat had increased speed by several knots.

"Well, I guess that extra oil made a difference after all." John smiled to himself as he propped his feet up.

As he put his hands behind his head, he noticed something odd out on deck. The lid to the crab hold cover was off.

"That's weird," John whispered to himself. "I could have sworn we covered that before we went inside."

He got up and walked outside to the deck and stood over the opening for the hold. Looking around, he noticed a strange clear-looking mucus covering the lid. Rain pelted the deck as John bent down and put the lid back on. The mucus covered his hand, giving it a sticky coating that took several wipes on his pants to remove. At first, he thought it was slime from jellyfish, but if that were the case, his hand would be on fire from the tentacle stings.

John put the thought in the back of his mind as he walked back to the wheelhouse to finish his shift. Lighting a cigarette, he eased back into the chair for the final time as he sipped on his coffee, praying it would help keep him awake.

As the hours passed by, the thought of the mysterious slime crept back into his head. What the hell could have made that stuff, and why was it also on the lid to the crab hold? Pondering the questions in his head, he looked out across the deck and thought he saw something moving on the railing. He leaned closer to the window as he made out what appeared to be a red snake coming across the rail. John wiped his eyes to make sure he wasn't dreaming, there was no way a snake would be out here.

Just as he was about to grab a pair of binoculars, the door behind him opened as Mike walked in. John turned around, taking his attention from the strange creature outside to look at the weary deck boss.

"What are you doing up here, Mike?" John asked as he turned back around, and found the creature was not there anymore.

"I couldn't sleep. I guess I'm so tired I'm awake. I figured since I can't sleep, you would enjoy being relieved early to get some extra rest," Mike answered him.

"Uh, thanks, man," John replied as he brought the binoculars to his eyes and scanned outside. Finding nothing, he began to debate if what he thought he saw was even real.

Mike looked at him with a confused look. "What are you looking at, John?"

"I could have sworn I saw something outside, something on the rail."

"What was it?" Mike asked him.

"Call me crazy but it looked kinda like a big snake going across the deck. It had a reddish color and was going over the rail. Hell, I must be tired, don't listen to me."

Mike stopped in his tracks as the words flooded through his brain, making him think about what he had seen on the camera footage from the night of Travis' disappearance.

"How long ago did you see it?" Mike asked.

"It was right before you walked in, but it's not there anymore. I'm tired, it was probably just my imagination," John reassured him.

Standing up, John grabbed his cup of coffee and started to walk towards the door before Mike stopped him.

"What's on your pants, John?" Mike asked in an alarmed tone.

"Oh, just some kind of slime that was out on deck. I guess we left the lid to the crab hold open, so I went and put it back on, and this slime was covering it. I figured it was from some old jellyfish or something," he replied.

Mike thought about it, unable to shake the fact that things were getting stranger by the minute on this boat. "We're too far north to be around any schools of jellyfish... there was slime on the rail where Travis went overboard."

The blood rushed out of John's face. "You think it's connected? The slime?"

"Not just the slime, but all of it," Mike told him. "The slime, the red rope around Travis, the red snake you just saw; I think it's all connected somehow. Connected to what, I don't know."

"We need to tell the captain about what's been happening, have him turn the boat around. The left engine is on its last leg, and if something is going on, I'd like to start heading home while we still have both engines." The level of concern in John's voice was beginning to rise.

"I don't know if he'd believe us, man. He's got the taste of crab now, short of the boat sinking there isn't anything that will convince him to leave now. Not until we got the tanks full, and we need to offload. There's something he hasn't told the rest of the crew yet." Mike looked down in defeat because he knew they were stuck out here until Captain Wilder was ready to leave.

John looked at Mike with curiosity. "What's that?"

"He's got cancer." Mike answered him. "He's using this trip as a last gamble to get some money before he leaves the fishing business. Cap is gonna give me the boat after this season is over. The way it's going... if we make it back from this season."

"Well, that's some good news for a change. I'm glad you're the one that's gonna be up here in the seat from now on. We just need to make it through this trip. At least the fishing is going well though," John chuckled.

"Listen, you should head to bed. Keep what we just talked about between us, we don't need everyone else on the boat going into a panic, you know how superstitious some of them are. Just keep your eyes open for any other strange shit and let me know. I'll do what I can to get the captain to turn around but I doubt he'll listen to me." Mike took the seat at the wheel and ushered John out the door.

John turned and looked at Mike before he opened the door. "Do you think it could be one of the crew? Someone sabotaging our boat?"

Mike shook his head. "I doubt it, we would have seen them doing something by now. And there's no reason for anyone to ruin everything since we're all here trying to make money. I think something else is going on. I don't know, but I think it all has something to do with Travis getting pulled off the boat."

"Pulled off, you mean like something grabbed him?" John asked.

"I think at this point it's a possibility," Mike answered without a hint of emotion, staring out the large window to the deck.

John shook his head with confusion. "But what could pull a full-grown man like Travis off the boat, way out here in the middle of nowhere?"

"I have no idea, man," Mike told him. "Just keep your eyes open when you're out on deck. I don't want to lose anyone else with all this weird shit going on."

John nodded as he walked out the door. "I'll keep both open. Goodnight, Mike."

Sitting alone, Mike tried to think of what he could say to the captain to convince him to turn the boat around, but he couldn't think of anything. It would take a force of nature to make that man want to go home with the crew pulling numbers of six to nine hundred crab per pot.

One thought stayed in Mike's mind the rest of the night however, John saying that the crab container lid was off. Mike was the last man on deck, and personally put the lid on himself before turning in. The lid wasn't light, so being bumped off by rough seas was a very unlikely answer, and the rest of the crew hadn't left the ship since they turned in for the night.

Mike sat and went through his mind to try and figure out an answer to his questions. But the more he thought, the more questions that came to his mind. He made the decision that tomorrow, after they hauled their last string, he would convince Captain Wilder that they needed to turn around and go home.

Mike exhaled a breath of relief, knowing that after one more shift of hauling pots, they would be going home, even with a little bit of money for a change. He didn't know how he was going to convince the captain, but by any means, the boat was going to be going home. All they had to do was pray nothing went wrong for a few more days. Luckily, Mike was feeling optimistic and smiled.

CHAPTER NINE:

A phone call rang in the captain's quarters, breaking Tom Wilder from his deep sleep. He rolled over and picked the phone up to answer it. "Yeah."

"Hey Cap, it's Justin, just wanted to let you know we are gonna be coming up on the first pot in a few minutes. The crew is all ready to go, just waiting on your word to start."

Tom looked at the clock sitting on his nightstand, confused about how they could be coming up on the string already. They should have another five hours before they reached their pots, not five minutes. With the added weight of the crab they had on board, the boat wasn't able to go as fast as she could usually travel.

"I'll be right up... something's not right." Captain Wilder hung the phone up and got his fishing clothes on and proceeded to the wheelhouse. He stopped by the galley and grabbed a mug full of coffee that was waiting for him on the counter. Walking up the stairs, he reached the door and turned the handle, seeing Justin sitting in the chair, eager to be relieved.

"What do you mean we're already at the first-string, Justin?" the old captain asked.

Justin stood nervously, trying to think if there was something that he'd done wrong. "I mean we're here, Cap. I can see the first buoy about half a mile ahead. We've been on autopilot all night, following the course you set before turning in. The boat's been going at full speed, we made good time getting here."

Captain Wilder shook his head with the mention of their speed. "That's impossible, we have over 63,000 pounds of crab on board, we should be dragging ass getting here, not be ahead of schedule."

"I don't know what to tell ya, boss, we haven't touched any of the controls and nothing crazy has happened all night. Well, Mike said the left engine's been acting up and the crab hold lid was left open for a while last night."

"That's odd, I could have sworn Mike closed it up before he left. And if the engine's acting up, that would have screwed with our speed. Have one of the guys go and check the crab hold, make sure they're still in there. Just to be sure," Tom ordered Justin.

"Ok, boss, I'll have Mitchell check it out," Justin replied.

******

What a way to start the fishing day, Mitchell thought to himself, checking the crab tank when they already know the crab are in there. Walking with a flashlight in hand, he sulked his way to the lid and used all his strength to open it. Turning on the light, he bent down and flashed the beam into the tank.

The flashlight dropped from his hand as Mitchell stood frozen in shock, his mouth completely open. This was impossible, there was no way he was seeing what he was looking at. He raced to the nearest speaker and began yelling into it, "Captain, you need to get down here NOW!!!"

******

Captain Wilder stood at the crab hold in complete shock and confusion. The rest of the crew stood around him as they couldn't believe their eyes: the tank was empty.

"How the hell do over sixty thousand pounds of crab just go missing??!" the captain yelled. "This tank was full yesterday when we went to sleep!!"

John looked at him in complete confusion. "I don't know, man, like I told you earlier, the only thing that happened was the lid was off, but I went and put it back on. I didn't notice any crab on the deck. Just some slime on the lid."

Captain Wilder's temper flared. "Oh yeah, because some jellyfish just climbed on top of the boat, opened the thirty-pound lid, and started sneaking the crab off the boat while we were all sleeping. You fucking MORON!!"

Mike felt the need to intervene for how the captain was taking his frustration out on the crew. "Hey Tom, take it easy, he's just telling you what he saw. We're all pretty upset about what Mitchell found today. But yelling at everyone isn't gonna change what happened."

Kyle looked at the hold and inspected it for any clues as to what could have happened.

"Maybe there's a hole in the tank and they all crawled out as we kept driving. That'd be a logical explanation for what happened," Kyle explained.

John shook his head. "Not a chance, if there was a hole anywhere on the boat we would be sitting at the bottom of the ocean by now. And there isn't enough water towards the top of the tank for the crab to be able to crawl out."

"I guess this explains why we were picking up speed last night instead of slowing down, we lost sixty thousand pounds of weight," Mitchell muttered in a low voice.

Tom walked to the nearest bucket and kicked it as hard as he could. "FUCKKKKKK!! DAMN IT!!!"

He ran to the rail and started kicking the deck boards in frustration and yelling every obscenity he could think of. The crew stood, looking in every direction but at the captain, who despite being older, was doing an excellent job at cracking the boards with his feet.

"Every time something goes right, ten things go wrong!!" Tom screamed as loud as he could.

Mike told the crew to head inside and finish getting ready for the upcoming shift. He watched as his friend began coughing again, doubling over as blood came from his mouth. Tom stayed there for a moment until the coughing spat was done and tried to regain his breath. He stood up and stared out at the sea, the sun staying slightly above the horizon.

"We better hope this string pays off as good as that first one did, or we're in deep shit, man. I'm out of ideas for where to go next if this spot doesn't pan out," Captain Wilder said in a low tone, wiping his mouth with his sleeve.

Mike looked down; he didn't know the right words to say to him, knowing how much the captain had riding on his last trip to sea. He wanted to tell him that they needed to turn around and go home but didn't have the heart to kick him while he was down. "We'll think of something, Tom. If we have to, we can prospect a little bit, throw some random pots all around and see where the crab are at. If we have to, we'll grind on low numbers until we get these tanks full."

Tom chuckled as he listened to the deck boss, knowing that was the same thing he would have said if the roles were reversed. "I think you're gonna make a great captain, Mike, that's the best answer anyone can give to a problem like we're having."

He walked over to Mike and put his hand on his shoulder. "Get the guys ready and let's get this done. And pray that these pots come up full."

******

The waves crashed violently over the side of the rail as the first set of pot buoys came into view. Captain Wilder angled the boat perfectly to give John a clean throw, letting him land the throw on the first try. Once he got the line in the block, all the crew waited in anticipation to see what the bounty would be for the crab hungry crew. The line continued rolling up into the block, every foot that passed through was another foot closer to more money.

John stood, counting the feet of line in anticipation for the pot to finally clear the water's edge. When he judged that there was five feet of line left, he gave the signal for Mitchell and Justin to get ready to grab the pot.

Three feet of line...

Justin and Mitchell waited in anticipation. Captain Wilder's eyes were glued to the window, praying that the pot would come up like the last string.

One foot of line...

The top of the pot slowly came up over the waves, and before the crew could hold on to another second of hope, the bottom of the pot was hanging over the sea, completely empty.

The captain and crew's hearts sank down to their stomachs; this pot was a blank. Over the next several hours, as pot after pot came up the side empty, the men's morale sank lower than ever before. They had gotten the taste of a season where they would come out on top and now those dreams were becoming a nightmare.

"Come on, big man," Captain Wilder said, looking up at the sky. "Give me a little something to work with, that's all I'm asking."

******

After thirty empty pots had been hauled, John threw the hook once more, and as the line was running in the block, he could tell that something was wrong. The block was pulling the line up faster than it should be, indicating something more serious than just an empty pot. Suddenly, the end of the line went through the crab block, with no pot attached to the end of it.

Mike looked at John, confused about what had happened to the eight hundred pound crab pot. "What the hell happened? How'd we lose it?"

"I don't know, man," John yelled back to him. "Maybe the line was bad and rotted while it was sitting down there. All I know is the captain's gonna be pissed."

Turning to look at the greenhorn, Mike yelled to him, "I thought I told you to check all of the lines before we left, man!"

"I did, they were all good! I had to replace five but that was it, all the rest looked almost brand new," Kyle told him as he put his hands up. "Maybe the knot came undone as it was being pulled up."

John inspected the end of the line. "The knot didn't come undone, the end is all frayed, like it was torn off."

The hair on the back of Mike's neck stood up; nothing was strong enough in the ocean to tear the line apart from a crab pot.

"Let's hope this is the only one like this," Mike told the rest of the crew. "'Cause if we have any more like this, we're in deep shit. "

The crew got back to their positions and waited for the next set of buoys to come into sight. Once the two orange buoys were in sight, Captain Wilder positioned the boat for the perfect throwing angle for the engineer. When they were within mere feet, John threw the hook with all of his might and landed it perfectly once again.

Putting the line into the block, John was relieved to watch as the rope holding the pot was racing at its usual speed, indicating that this pot was not lost. While a slower moving line would mean a full pot, he would settle for just having an intact one right now.

As the pot rose above the water, the entire crew's jaws dropped as they saw something none of them had ever seen before. Mike maneuvered the crane and set the pot on the launcher, activating the dog legs to secure it, and walked over to inspect it.

All of the meshing on the pot was gone, leaving just the metal frame sitting there in the launcher, the bait was gone. Any part of the pot that was not metal had been removed, leaving no trace that it was even there to begin with. If something large had been caught in the mesh, it would have just torn it in places, but this was something else.

"What the fuck is going on?" Mike asked aloud to no one in particular.

Suddenly, John's voice called him over, "Hey Mike... you need to see this."

Mike went over to him and leaned in to look at what John had discovered and was completely dumbfounded by what he saw.

The entire shell of the pot was covered with small holes, like a pack of metal eating fish had had a feeding frenzy on it for the past few days. The two men looked at each other, trying to figure out what could have done this.

"What do you think, Mike? Salt water erosion on the metal?" John asked him.

The corner of Mike's mouth twitched as he thought of his own answer. "Yeah, maybe if this pot had been sitting at the bottom for twenty years. We put this pot down only days ago, and it looks like it got dropped in an acid bath. Nothing I know of can do something like this."

"Hey, look at this..." Kyle pointed to the back of the half-existing crab pot, to a clear liquid; thick, and slime-like.

John was the first to put his fingers in it and rolled it around his hand. He thought back to the night before, where he encountered a similar substance on the crab tank lid.

"This is the same stuff that was on the tank lid, when I was out on deck last night," John muttered to the men around him. "What's it doing on the pot?"

Mike brought his hand down to the unknown substance and felt it as well. "And it's the same as the stuff on the railing where Travis went over."

"Ok, I'm officially sketched out now, guys," Justin stammered, his hands beginning to shake with anxiety. "What the hell could destroy a crab pot like that?"

"I don't know, but we're not gonna wait around to find out." Mike turned and headed straight for the wheelhouse. "We're turning this boat around and going home."

******

"Like hell we're gonna turn this boat around, Mike!" Captain Wilder yelled. "I get being superstitious, but this is ridiculous!"

"Tom, you have to turn the boat around!" Mike yelled back at him. "Something dangerous is going on out here, I don't know what exactly, but it's not worth the money anymore. We should have turned back the night we lost Travis."

Wilder looked at him with increasing anger, expecting this reaction from the rest of the crew, but not him. "People die in this job all the time, Mike, and they never turned around. You all see some jellyfish slime and think there's some kind of unusual explanation for everything going on. It's just been some bad luck, is all. We aren't leaving until we get our quota of crab and our money in our pockets"

He couldn't believe his ears. The words making him think of his longtime friend as no more than Captain Ahab, except instead of a white whale, he was chasing money. He moved in closer, hoping to talk some sense into him by telling him what he saw on the camera.

"I never got a chance to tell you, but I saw something when I was reviewing the footage from the deck, after Travis died. It showed something, Tom."

The captain rolled his eyes. "And what did it show, Mike? The Loch Ness monster pulling him in?"

The anger built even greater inside Mike. "No, but something pulled him into the water. He went overboard well after the pot buoys were already gone. And then that slime we found on the pot just now, I found the same shit on the rail where Travis was. And John found some on the tank lid last night. Not to mention, Tom, the fucking pot looks like it's been melted. Something is out here!"

Tom laughed the hardest he ever laughed before, nearly falling out of his chair. Coughing, the captain wiped his mouth. "You guys are something else, I swear. Listen, I could give you a long, drawn out reason to why we are going to stay out here and fish, but instead, I'll keep it short for you, Mike. We have a quota to catch, and I'm the captain. Conversation over. Get back out on deck and tell the guys any more talk of sea monsters or whatever you guys think is going on, and you forfeit your pay. Either way, you're gonna work until the tanks are full."

The years of friendship suddenly felt like it meant nothing. Mike was at a loss for words. The man that he had grown to respect and admire had become the person that gave captains a bad reputation, one that put the money before his crew.

"We've been friends a long time, Tom, and you've been my skipper for even longer. I've followed every order you've given me and never went against you. Even for this trip, I had your back and helped get the crew onboard to go. But this, this is crazy, we need to get out of here and go home."

Captain Wilder stood out of his chair and got within an inch from the deck boss' face, the smell of coffee and cigarettes hitting Mike like a train. "We go home... when the tanks are full. I don't care if a kraken climbs on this boat, we aren't leaving empty handed. Now get out there."

Mike turned, walked towards the door and stopped before turning the handle. "When we get back to port, if we get back to port, keep your fucking boat. I'm not gonna have this crew's blood on my hands for your retirement." And slammed the door behind him.

******

Mike walked out on deck and informed the crew that they would be staying at sea until the tanks were full. The men voiced their concerns and disapproval, even Justin, who was beginning to think that maybe he had been too hasty with his accusations.

"He can't do this, we need to turn around," Justin proclaimed. "Maybe we should just wait until he goes to sleep and turn the boat around ourselves."

Mike shot the idea down. "No, we do it the hard way, and keep fishing until we can go home. Everyone keep an eye open for each other and let me know if you see anything strange. We do that, we should be fine. Does Harvey know any of what's been going on?"

John shook his head. "No, he's been in the galley so much I hardly ever see him. I'll fill him in with what's been going on though next time I run into him."

Suddenly, Captain Wilder's voice screamed from the speaker onto the deck, "John, get to the engine room NOW!! I just lost power to the left engine!!"

"Oh shit," John yelled as he raced off the deck and down into the engine room.

******

As soon as John opened the door, gray smoke burned his eyes as he coughed and slowly tried making his way through the room. Years of being in this room helped him create a mental layout, giving him a natural compass to the engines. He could barely see, indicating to him that the engine was in dire condition.

Finally, he was able to reach the left engine, and it was in worse shape than he imagined. Oil was spurting from every valve that came out of it, smoke poured from both ends, and the belt had melted off from the heat. John knew there was no way to save it and reached for the phone that held a direct line to the wheelhouse.

The captain's voice answered, "How bad is it, John?"

"I have to shut the engine off, Cap, she's done. We're lucky a fire didn't break out from all the heat and oil this thing is putting off. The whole engine room is smoked out," John yelled back into the receiver, trying to outmatch the noise in the room.

'Fuck!!" Captain Wilder yelled. "Ok, fine. But you do whatever you have to do to keep that other engine alive. If not we're gonna be dead in the water out here."

"Will do. We're gonna have to have the whole engine replaced when we get back to port, she's well beyond an overhaul now, man. It's gonna be slow going though running on one engine," John informed him.

"I know, but we don't have a choice. Once we get these pots picked up and go back to where we set our first string, we're gonna start setting them again. We don't have the time or money to run back for a new engine."

John gave him an ok as he hung the phone up and went to work shutting the engine down. Once that was done, he propped the door to the room open and set up fans to get the smoke out and cleaned up the gallons of oil that was lying on the floor. Their situation just went from bad to worse.

Mike walked through the door, coughing as he went to the engineer, "How bad is it, John? Is it salvageable?"

"She's fucked, Mike," John replied. "We're only gonna be able to run the right engine for the rest of the trip until we get a new one. It's gonna be slow going, and it doesn't sound like the captain is gonna make a run for a new one. He's talking about heading back to our first string and resetting there."

"Things just went from bad to worse then, man," Mike remarked. "You sure there's nothing you can do to get it running again? What about keeping it filled with fresh oil?"

John threw the wrench he had in his hand to the ground, massaging his eyes with his hand. Being the only man on the boat that knew anything about engines had finally taken its toll on him. "Don't you think I already thought about that, Mike? The valves are busted and all the seals on the engine are blown. At this point, any oil you put in will be sitting on the floor before the can's empty. She's done."

Mike put his hands up, realizing he had struck a nerve. "Hey, I'm sorry, John. I know you've been busting your ass trying to keep it alive. We'll just have to make do with what we have until we get back to the harbor. How's the other engine doing?"

Rubbing his chin, John gave him a look of a combination of hope and doubt. "I don't know, Mike, the captain's gonna be running her harder than he should since we're staying out to fish. That's a lot to ask from a single engine, not to mention if we get back on the crab, we're gonna have a hell of an amount of weight to be pushing around."

John reached into his pocket and lit a fresh cigarette, letting his arms rest on the dead engine as he stared at the ceiling. Just when they thought this job was hard enough, another curve ball had to come across the plate. John inhaled the smoke as he pondered if it was worth trying to convince the captain to turn back, but he knew that was going to be a waste of breath.

"You sure you should be smoking with all this oil and shit around?" Mike asked, trying to break the silence.

John slowly blew the smoke out of his mouth and gave him a smile. He adjusted his ballcap on his head and gave him a simple answer, "Mike, at this point, I don't give a fuck. We're in deep shit and we just lost our shovel."

Mike patted him on the shoulder. "Hang in there, man, we're gonna get through this. Just do everything you can for the engine and let me worry about everything else."

Giving him a nod, John flicked the butt of his cigarette into a metal coffee can. "Well, I guess it's not like things can get a whole lot worse." John laughed as he walked through the door to go back out on deck and help the rest of the crew prepare the crab pots for setting.

CHAPTER TEN:

The squid sensed something different about the creature swimming along the water, for some reason it had slowed down considerably. It concluded that the creature must have been wounded somehow, causing confusion since no other predator had been seen by the beast. The senses heightened with the thought of another predator in the water, causing it to swim in a circle underneath it.

Once it concluded that there were no other animals around, it knew that now was the time to strike. With the creature wounded, bringing it down would be a simpler job, and it had the element of surprise. Its massive tentacles trailed behind it as it began swimming towards the surface, performing a circular pattern to keep its prey from knowing the angle in which it would strike from.

The hunger was setting in quickly, the desire to feed and replenish the energy that was gone from its body. The thought of food was driving it into a frenzy, the madness taking over again as it loomed closer and closer to the surface. The sensors on the appendages indicated there were creatures moving about on its prey. More food for the hungry monster.

******

The crew worked hard as they kept pulling the rest of their crab pots from the ocean, or what was left of the pots. Every single pot had been destroyed, leaving only the buoy line and buoys left to show that there was once gear there. All of the morale on the boat had been completely diminished, there was now only a little over one hundred pots left to try and catch the rest of their quota. With each pot that came up, Captain Wilder screamed another profanity across the deck through the speakers.

The water had finally calmed, the sun sitting high and without the hinderance of clouds. The crew had the privilege of working in the sun for a change and enjoyed it while they could; weather had a habit of changing quickly. Mike leaned his head over the rail and looked to see how many pots they had left before they were finished. His heart sank as he could see buoys as far as his eyes could see; they still had more than an hour and a half worth of work ahead of them.

Harvey walked out on deck moments later, a plate full of sandwiches in his hand, and a smile on his face. "Hey fellas, break time! I cleared it with the captain and he said you guys could grab a bite to eat. I figured you would want to eat out here since it's such a nice day out."

Justin gave his usual smart remark. "Yeah Harvey, that's just what we wanted, eat our food with the smell of rotten cod fish all around."

He felt a shove from behind, spinning around only to see Mike standing behind him, giving him a look that made him back down instantly. Mike was clearly not in the mood for any attitude today. "Just shut up and take a sandwich, Justin. I've had more than enough of your mouth for one day."

John laughed as he took a sandwich from the plate and eyed it to see the contents. Roast beef and Swiss, one of the crew's favorite breaktime snacks. As he walked over to find a seat so he could eat, he felt a bump from the bottom of his feet, like the boat had hit a pothole.

"Anyone else feel that?" he asked aloud.

"Oh probably just ran over a walrus or something, you know how the captain gets when he's on a crunch for time." Harvey laughed. "He doesn't care what's in his way, he'll run it over when it comes to fishing. Hell, I saw him drive the boat over a school of Marlin when I fished with him down south years ago. Didn't care 'cause they weren't the fish he was after, and they were in his way."

John shuddered. "Man, that's cold. I know a lot of people that would kill just to find a single Marlin, let alone an entire school."

"Yeah, took us two days to clean the blood off the bottom of the boat. That stuff sticks like chum, and smells like it too," Harvey laughed.

All of a sudden, a wall of water showered over the rail and doused the crew. Sandwiches went flying and most of the crew were knocked off their feet, except for Harvey, who had kept his balance. This time, it clearly wasn't a walrus.

The men looked up and stared in horror as massive red tentacles hung above the boat, waving back and forth as if they had eyes of their own, searching for prey. None of the men dared move, they were paralyzed with fear. The plate in Harvey's hand shook uncontrollably as one of the tentacles slithered in the air towards him. He began walking backwards as it came closer to him, the giant suction cups flaring out as the tip of it made a cup shape, as if to form a hand.

"No.. No.. Please No!!" Harvey cried as he continued backwards, unable to do much else. No one on deck helped him as the tentacle grabbed Harvey by the waist and picked him up into the air.

The squid held him fifteen feet above the deck as it began constricting, breaking several of his ribs. Harvey screamed and coughed as the air was forced out of his lungs, his legs kicking as he begged it to let him go. A second, thinner tentacle swept through the air and coiled itself underneath the larger one. The two pulled in opposite directions, and everyone on deck heard the popping sound of Harvey's spine being pulled apart.

Feeling an extreme amount of pain followed by the feeling of nothingness, all Harvey could do was allow his limp, paralyzed body to be at the whim of the giant monster. Feeling like he was trapped in his own body, he couldn't feel pain, but could feel the terror as the tentacle cocked him back and slammed him headfirst into the deck boards.

While he couldn't feel the pain, he knew he was dying as the tentacle picked him up and he could see chunks of white skull and pieces of brain matter lying on the deck. Again, the tentacle slammed him head first, his head cracking open completely and spilling the rest of what was in his skull outwards. A piece of Harvey's brain hit Justin in the face, causing him to vomit all over himself.

Mike was the first to break the silence and screamed, "Everyone inside now!!!" He picked himself up and began running for the door, dodging a tentacle that came sweeping overhead. Justin and Mitchell crawled as fast as they could to get inside, a red tentacle twisting around Justin's leg and trying to pull him over the railing. Mitchell looked over at him as Justin began screaming for help and pulled a small fishing knife out of his pocket. He crawled back to him and, knife in hand, began stabbing the tentacle as hard as he could, his hand becoming covered in clear slime.

The squid let go of the deckhand and made a whipping motion, throwing Mitchell several feet, forcing the knife out of his hand. He looked down at his hand and realized Mike had been right all along, the slime was the proof. Grabbing Justin, who was hyperventilating from panic, they made their way to the door and continued inside.

Mike finally reached the door as Justin and Mitchell ran in. He turned around and helped Kyle to his feet and shoved him through the doorway. Taking a mental count of the crew, he realized he was a man short, John was still out on deck. The engineer was standing out in the middle, yelling at the monster as it waved the body of his friend in the air.

"Give him back, you SON OF A BITCH!!!" John yelled. Tears ran down his face as he watched Harvey's body flail like a rag doll, becoming a toy for the squid to play with.

Mike ran to him as the tentacles started to crawl closer to John. Grabbing him by the shirt, he started pulling him back towards the ready room. "John, come on, we need to get out of here!"

"We can't leave Harvey, Mike!! We have to get him back!" John screamed as he fought the deck boss to stay where he was. "I think he's still alive!"

"No one could have survived that, man!" Mike yelled back at him as he slowly pulled him into the ready room. "We need to find a way to get this thing away from the boat or it's gonna sink us!"

All of a sudden, the tentacles retracted back into the ocean, except for the one holding on to the ship's cook. The tentacle gave one final pummel of his body into the deck boards, slowly dragging him to the rail.

Guilt once again formed in Mike's throat as he watched his limp body being dragged overboard. He could tell most of his bones had been broken by the way Harvey's body rolled over the rail like he was made of water. And in the next instant, he was taken into the sea.

Eyes watering, Mike walked through the door. "He's gone." And shut the door behind him.

******

He couldn't believe his eyes, a sea monster had just killed Harvey and had attacked the boat. Captain Wilder panicked and pushed the throttle down as far as it would go, hoping to escape the squid. The only problem though was in his panic, he failed to realize a set of buoys were right in the way of the boat. As the boat passed over the line, the propeller became tangled in the buoys, bringing the boat to a slow stop. A yellow caution light began flashing on the instrument panel, indicating they were in serious trouble.

"What the fuck is going on now?" he asked himself. "As if we don't have enough going on."

Looking down at his speedometer, he noticed their speed was sitting at zero. He looked over at his computer and noticed the position of the boat was sitting right over where he had set one of his pots. "Oh shit."

Picking up the intercom mic, he made an announcement to the crew, "Everyone meet in the galley right now!"

As much as he pushed the remaining engine, the boat wasn't going anywhere. The buoy line was completely constricting the propeller and the only thing he was able to do was push the throttle, but the prop wouldn't move an inch. He slammed his fist down onto the table. "Damn it!!!"

The anger in the old captain began boiling through his head, sending him into a rampage as he began destroying everything within arm's reach. In his blinding rage, he grabbed their only working radio and threw it on the ground, stomping it to a thousand pieces.

******

The remainder of the crew sat silently at the table in the galley, except for Justin, who had stopped by his room on his way to the meeting. No one said a word as they digested what had happened, mourning over the loss of their friend, and debating what to do with the fact that there was a sea monster hunting them.

John finally broke the silence, "What the hell was that out there?"

"I think it was a squid of some kind," Mike replied. "Judging by the tentacles that were all over the boat."

"That's impossible though, Mike," Mitchell chimed in, his hands shaking as he tried to take a drink out of his cup. "Squid don't get that big, and this thing looks as big as our boat. Did you see the size of those tentacles?"

"I'm just calling it as I see it, man. It's got tentacles so it could either be a big ass squid, or a giant octopus. It doesn't exactly matter which it is, the key thing is we're in deep shit." Mike looked over at Mitchell and noticed a substance on his hand. "What's on your hand, Mitchell?"

He took a towel off the table and started wiping his hand to get the slime off. "Oh, when I grabbed one of the tenacles to get Justin free, it was covered in this nasty ass slime. I thought I got most of it off, but this shit's thick."

The wheels in Mike's head started to turn as all the pieces to the puzzles from the last few days finally came together. "This thing has been following us for days."

"How do you know that?" Justin asked as he walked in from his room. John thought he noticed a slight stumble in his step as he sat down. But there was no way Justin could think about drinking at a time like now, John thought to himself, dismissing the accusation.

"Well, every time something has happened on this boat on this trip, that slime has been there. From Travis going overboard, to the crab tank being empty. And then we found that same shit on that crab pot earlier today, this thing must have been what destroyed them and killed Travis." The crew went silent, everyone pondering if this was just some bad dream they were having. This was something out of a horror movie, not what happens on an average fishing trip. Mike looked around at all of their faces, they were all scared; he didn't blame them at all, hell he was scared more than he had ever been in his life. But he knew that they needed someone to pull them through this and think of a solution to their problem.

Kyle chimed up, breaking the silence, "Has anyone seen the captain?"

Mike hadn't realized Captain Wilder was nowhere to be seen. "He's probably in the wheelhouse still, someone's got to keep the boat going so we can get out of here and hopefully he's calling someone for help."

******

Tom Wilder held the broken pieces of radio in his hands, still shaking from the anger pulsing through his veins. He cursed himself; if he had been thinking clearly, he wouldn't have destroyed their only life line of getting someone to help them. But then, he looked up and stared at the GPS, realizing the radio wouldn't have done them any good anyways.

The boat was hundreds of miles away from the nearest fishing vessel, and well out of radio range for the US Coast Guard. The only boat they had a hair's chance in communicating with would be a Russian vessel, but no one on the boat knew how to speak the language. They were completely on their own, with no chance of a rescue. The harbor wouldn't think anything was wrong until months down the road, when the fishing season was finally concluded. By that time, they would all be sitting in the stomach of whatever the hell was attacking them.

He stood up and walked over to his captain's journal and looked at the fishing numbers over the last few days. The spot where they were at was a graveyard, but their first spot he had picked was a gold mine. An idea grew in his head, as a cruel grin formed across his face. Leaving the wheelhouse, he made his way to his quarters and shut the door behind him. Getting on one knee, he struggled and pulled a metal case from underneath his bed. Using his key ring, he unlocked it and opened the cover.

He stared with joy as his Remington 700 was where he had left it at the beginning of the trip. He kept the rifle in his cabin in case any kind of pirate or lunatic thought his boat was a free meal ticket. Tom picked it up and ran the bolt back and forth a couple of times. Satisfied that the action was working properly, he opened it again and began putting the 180 grain bullets into the chamber. Once he loaded the fifth one in, he closed the bolt and polished the glass on the 2x-7x scope sitting on top of it.

He reached back into the case and pulled out all the boxes of ammunition he had and lay them on the table. He bit on his lip as he debated if he would have enough bullets to kill the monster. Dumping the rounds out, he counted sixty, and put them into a pouch that could be worn around the waist. He slung the rifle over his shoulder and began walking to the galley, where he would have to break the news that someone was going to have to cut the line out from the propellers. Someone was going to have to go in the water.

CHAPTER ELEVEN:

Sitting at the table, Mike tried to think of a logical explanation for how a creature this size was currently living out here in the Bering Sea. The only other large animal that he knew could survive out here were seals, and the only threat they posed was if they bumped into the propeller. He looked at Mitchell, his hands still shaking as he smoked another cigarette to try and calm his nerves.

"Where the hell's the captain at? He should have been down here by now," John said, looking at his watch. "We need to come up with a game plan to get out of here. That thing probably isn't gonna wait much longer before it tries to take another go at us."

Justin crossed his hands in front of his mouth and spoke with a very low tone. "You know, my dad told me stories a long time ago about a creature out here. I thought he was just trying to keep me from being on a boat, but I think he was right. He said something lived out here that could tear a boat in half and eat a man in one bite."

Mitchell's hands began to shake worse than ever. "You think this is the creature he was talking about?" His tone was quivering with fear.

John spit his coffee out as he began to laugh. "Justin, what the hell are you talking about? I knew your dad, he was a drunk that spent every dollar he had at the bar and made up stories to naive boaters to make them think he was a big shot. I heard him tell some kid that his grandfather was crab fishing where the Titanic sank and he helped some of those people on the lifeboats get to safety. He'd say anything if it meant someone would buy him a drink. And it looks like the apple didn't fall far from the tree."

Justin lunged across the table and grabbed him by the collar. "You keep my dad out of your mouth, you piece of shit! He was more a crabber than you will ever be!"

Dishes and cups flew from the table as both men fought, everyone else trying to get out of the way as the brawl went from bad to worse. John punched Justin in the throat, causing him to struggle to breathe. Grabbing the deckhand, John threw him across the table, causing him to roll as something flew out of his back pocket.

"What is that?" Mike asked.

John walked over and picked it up. Turning it over he realized what it was. "You're seriously drinking right now, you piece of shit?" He turned to the others and showed them what it was: a flask.

"What the fuck, Justin?" Mike yelled. "As if we don't have enough problems going on right now, you're drinking?"

John held the flask and shook it to gauge how much was left in it. "I'd say by how empty it is he must have a real nice buzz going. I thought I saw you stumble when you came in, and now I know I wasn't seeing shit." He tossed the flask onto Justin's stomach, making him flinch.

"Excuse me for trying to enjoy my last few hours alive before I'm eaten alive by a giant fucking monster," Justin wheezed, opening the lid and taking a long pull from it before sticking it back in his pocket.

Kyle walked over and helped him to his feet. Justin tried to keep his balance with the combination of booze and a throbbing head throwing his equilibrium off. Mike told all of them to sit back down at the table.

"Look, no one else is gonna die. We can get out of here, and that's what we're gonna do. From here on out no one goes outside, we should be safe here inside the galley. Both times that thing attacked, we were out there fishing. And as far as I'm concerned, there's no reason we can't stay inside until we make it back to port."

"That's where you're wrong..."

Everyone turned and saw Captain Wilder walk through the door, a rifle slung over his shoulder. He walked to the table and slammed the rifle down and the pouch full of ammunition.

"We got a big problem; one of the buoy lines is caught in the propeller," he informed them.

John put his head down in defeat, rubbing his face with his palms. "You gotta be kidding me." He brought his hands up and began running his fingers through his hair, a telltale sign of the stress he was feeling. "As if things couldn't get any worse."

"What does that mean?" Kyle asked, looking confused.

"It means that some line is wrapped around the propeller blade, like a coiled snake. As long as it's wrapped up, the propeller can't spin. In layman's terms, this boat won't go anywhere until that rope is taken off," John answered him.

"Well how do we do that?" Kyle asked him.

The room fell silent as no one wanted to say the words that they all knew were coming. Someone was going to have to get in the water and cut the rope by hand. Mitchell's hands began shaking worse than ever before, followed by his body shaking like an old rusted car.

"Someone is gonna have to go down there and cut the rope out," Captain Wilder directed, turning to look at Mitchell. "You brought your dive gear, right Mitch?"

Mitchell jumped up from the table in a panic, becoming borderline hysterical. "Ohhh no, I'm not going in there, man!! Nooo way in hell am I getting in that water with that thing down there!"

"Take it easy, bud." Mike tried calming him down. "It's gonna be ok, I'm sure there's another way. We can probably get some pole hooks and get it off."

Captain Wilder took control of the room. "No, that's gonna take too long, and that's even if it works." He walked to Mitchell and stuck his finger in his face. "I hired you because you're qualified as a diver, and guess what? We have a diving situation that's pretty damn serious. So put your gear on and get in the fucking water, Mitchell!"

"NOOO!!!" Mitchell screamed as he ran to his room, hugging the support pole that was in there as tight as humanly possible. "I'm not going down there, and you can't make me!! I'm not gonna die like Travis and Harvey!"

Mike could hear crying coming from the room. He felt pity for him, everyone knew that the only person that could go in the water was Mitchell. But Mike couldn't imagine the fear that must be going through his mind. The creature had already killed two of them, one in the most horrific manner he had ever seen. And now the captain was ordering him to go into the water where that thing lived.

"Get out here, you son of a bitch!" Captain Wilder yelled as he walked to the room.

Mike grabbed his arm and stopped him. "Hey, give him a break, Tom. Do you even realize what you're asking him to do? He's scared shitless and I don't blame him one bit. Yelling at him isn't gonna do anything but make things worse."

The anger in Wilder's eyes burned right through Mike as he ordered Mike to follow him out of the room. Once both men were in the outer hallway, Wilder looked to make sure the door was closed behind them.

"We don't have time for this shit, Mike," he growled to him. "He needs to get down there and cut us loose so we can get moving and kill this thing."

Mike looked at him with the same look a toddler would give a parent when asked to do an algebra equation. "What do you mean kill it? We just need to get out of there. If we get out of these fishing grounds, we can radio the coast guard and get some help."

Captain Wilder shook his head. "No, we can't Mike, the radio's broken. We have no way of calling for help from anyone."

"Well, we should have a spare radio. Give me a few minutes and I can get it hooked up for when we're able to get going."

"There is no spare, I sold it last season," Tom answered. "We don't have any spares for any of the electronics on the boat. I sold all of them."

"What do you mean there's no spares?" Mike asked in shock. "We're always supposed to have some kind of backup in case something like this happens. Now we're screwed! We have no way to reach anyone and get help."

Captain Wilder grabbed Mike by his shirt collar and threw him against the wall, turning into a form of monster Mike had never seen before. The veins on his face bulged as red began streaking across, showing the anger that had been brewing.

"I did it so you all could have a paycheck last season! Did you think that money just came out of thin air, huh?" Tom yelled at him.

"I sold everything that wasn't nailed down already so you sorry lot could pay your bills and go enjoy a drink at the bar. I walked away with nothing... but that's gonna change this season."

A grin formed across Tom's face that was a combination of madness and excitement and he refused to let go of his grip. For the first time, Mike didn't know what to do. He had never seen his captain like this before, a deranged man that was running out of options.

"We need to get out of here, man. If we convince Mitchell to dive down and cut that line free, we can turn around and go home. Maybe we can dump all of our bait in the water and give something to keep that creature occupied," Mike tried to reason.

Tom's grin became even wider. "I've got a better idea, Mike."

His heart sank as he prepared for what he had in mind.

"We're gonna kill the bastard!" Tom yelled at him. "You're gonna convince Mitchell to go in that water and get this boat going. I don't care what it takes, tell him he can have a double share if that's what it takes. Then we'll take that rifle and keep shooting that piece of shit until we're chopping him up and using him for crab bait!!"

"We don't even know if that will kill that thing, Tom! This is insane; what's going on with you?" Mike yelled back at him, trying to push him off of himself.

"Well, then we'll find a way, damn it. 'Cause I found where the crab are... I was on 'em, Mike. We kill this thing, we can go back to where we set that first string and make a fortune! And with less crew on board, your share will be even bigger." Wilder's grip became even tighter when the talk of crab came out of his mouth. "We're gonna make a fortune, the only thing standing in the way of that, is that fucking thing out there."

As the words went into Mike's ears, he could hear the madness becoming fully clear now. Trying not only to convince him to stay fishing but using the dead crew members as a way to put more money in his pocket. The man he used to call his friend was now truly gone, completely consumed by his drive for money.

"There's no way I'm gonna tell those guys that they have to go back out there, Tom. Not for any amount of money," Mike rebutted, doubting his words would have any chance of changing the captain's mind.

"Oh you're gonna convince them, Mike." The captain smiled to him. "'Cause if you don't, I'll throw you overboard myself and use you to lure that creature to us. So, you decide. Convince the rest to get on board or take a shot to the gut and be used for chum."

It was one of easiest decisions Mike had made in a long time, but how he was gonna go through with it, he had no idea. He'd have to get the crew, especially Mitchell, to follow this lunatic and find a way to kill this thing. Not to mention convince Mitchell to go into the water to free the boat. "I'll do it, I'll help you kill this thing."

!That's the spirit!" Tom chuckled as he let him go. "Now first thing's first. Tell that junkie to get his ass in that water so we can get this boat moving again."

Mike resisted the urge to wrap his hands around his neck, but he knew that if they wanted any chance of getting out of here, they would need all hands on deck. "I'll help you do this, Tom, but after this, I'm done. You can keep your boat and burn it to the ground for all I care. If I ever see you again, I swear on Harvey and Travis' souls I'll kill ya."

Tom leaned in and gave an answer that Mike would never have guessed. "I like the way you worded that, Mike, you're already in the mindset that we're gonna kill this thing. Maybe we have a chance after all." Tom patted Mike on the shoulder and started walking back to the galley and began preparations for their diver to go swimming.

CHAPTER TWELVE:

The tentacle attached to the squid brought the last remaining bit of meat to its beak. It savored the taste of the still twitching limb as energy began flowing through its tentacles, creating warmth that brought new life. This new prey was a peculiar one, they didn't try and fight back, all they had done was hide within the larger creature.

The squid shot its tentacles behind it as it began circling around the prey, trying to plan the next course of action. It dove to the bottom of the sea bed as it looked for any more prey that could help extinguish the hunger that never ceased. The only thing the squid wanted was to give one fatal attack so it could feast and travel to more prosperous lands. But while the smaller prey didn't fight, the larger creature might be waiting for its own time to strike.

It debated how much longer it could stand living on this meager diet but erred on the side of caution. One does not survive over one hundred years without learning to be cautious in these oceans, even if food was nowhere to be seen.

Spotting a small cluster of clams, it cupped two tentacle-fuls into its grip and closed them, turning them into a mashed paste of clam and sand. The awaiting beak opened as the tentacles brought the food into it, mashing the small creatures before swallowing, sand and all. The thought of the growing hunger began to drive it mad again, thrusting out its tentacles and pummeling the ocean floor over and over again. Sand started to float up into the sea, creating a hazy view that was almost impossible to see through. Once the fury was over, it settled down to the ocean bed and covered itself with layers of sand. The pigment in the skin began to change to a greyish brown. Now, it would rest, until its prey attempted to escape, and the creature would once again feast on flesh.

******

Mike walked back into the galley, seeing the rest of the crew where they originally were, and looked over to Mitchell's room. He was still there, refusing to move an inch, his body still shaking from the fear of going into the water. Kyle had tried to convince him that the amount of time in the water would only be a few minutes, but Mitchell didn't care.

"There's nothing you can say, man, I aint going in there," the only words that Kyle could get out of him.

Mike walked over to John and asked him how Mitchell was taking the news.

"How do you think he's taking it, Mike? The dude's scared shitless, and I don't blame him. That thing down there's killed Travis and Harvey already, and now we're telling him to go down where that thing lives."

Mike looked down and then to Mitchell's room. "Well we have to find a way to convince him, John. He's the only one on board that knows how to dive, and the wet suit is fitted for him."

"What's the plan after we're free though? We're getting out of here, right?" John asked.

"No, the captain wants us to stay here so we can kill the thing, and then he wants to finish the rest of the season. And he says if we don't, he'll shoot me and throw me overboard," Mike said in a low voice.

"This is crazy, man, we have no chance of killing that thing. What's his plan? Keep shooting it until it bleeds to death?"

"I don't know, John," Mike answered simply. "He's so delusional right now that might be his only plan. But I know one thing, we don't have any chance at all unless Mitchell cuts us loose."

Mike started walking to Mitchell's room. As soon as he cleared the doorway Mitchell grabbed the beam tighter. "I'm not going in the water, Mike. You guys can call me a coward, a junkie, whatever you want, I don't care. I'm not gonna get ripped to pieces like the rest of them."

Mike leaned down and squatted to his level, feeling compassion for what he was about to ask of him.

Mitchell looked up into Mike's eyes and stared crying. "Don't make me go in there, Mike."

"I can't imagine what's going through your mind right now, man, and how scared you are. I wish I could be the one to go in the water, that I could bear this burden, but I can't. You're the only one that can go in there, Mitchell, you're the only one of us that has a dive suit and the experience to go cut that line free. We need you."

Mitchell looked down towards the ground and shook his head. "I don't know if I can, Mike, I'm so scared. That thing's out there, waiting. It's like it's picking us off one by one, like it's stalking us."

"I'll have John at the rail watching with the rifle, and we'll tie the heaviest line we have onto you. If anything happens, we'll pull you back up, and John will shoot that thing and make it think twice about trying to take a grab out of any of us."

Mitchell just kept looking down as he debated if he had the nerve to go in there. Mike bent down closer to him until Mitchell had no choice but to look back at him.

"Sometimes the only way through hell is to just walk through it, Tommy." Mike looked him in the eyes as he uttered the words he had always lived by, at least since he started this line of work.

"You guys have never used my first name before," Mitchell replied. Suddenly, he realized that the words coming from his deck boss weren't just talk, but genuine. Mitchell had told Mike his first name when he first came onto the boat, but since that day, no one had ever used it.

"I've never forgotten who you are Tommy, and everything that you've overcome to be where you are now. We need you, brother, we're asking you to go into that water and cut the boat loose, so we can kill this thing. We can make it up to Travis and Harvey, for what they had to endure. I'm asking you, man, will you go down there?" Mike asked with empathy.

"Ok, I will."

******

Mitchell sat by the edge of the railing as he finished putting his flippers on his feet and gave his regulator another once over. John held the oxygen tank harness for him while he put his shoulders through the straps and tightened them snug. Looking down at his belt, he made sure he had all the items he was going to need: a flashlight, a knife, and the safety line that was attached to his waist. The line was almost two inches in diameter and attached to a D ring sewed into the belt fabric.

"You sure that line is gonna be strong enough in case you guys have to pull me out in a hurry?" Mitchell asked Mike.

Mike was attaching the safety line to the boat itself, after running the line through the coiler.

"Don't worry, Mitch, that line is tested for over 10,000 pounds, nothing short of a whale is gonna pull it apart. And I have it going through the coiler so if we need to get you out of there fast, all I'll have to do is turn it on and you're back on the boat. Just try and watch your head as you're coming up."

Mitchell's voice was shaky as the time started to shorten for him. "Ok, good. You got that rifle loaded, John?"

John padded the buttstock of the hunting rifle slung over his shoulder. "Don't worry, she's good to go. As soon as you go in, I'll be standing over the side keeping an eye out for that thing. So much as a suction cup comes out of the water and it's gonna feel hot lead."

Mike looked out onto the ocean. The seas were calm today, and the sun shining bright, hopefully a sign of luck for them. He double checked the knot to the line on the boat. Once he was satisfied it was secure, he walked over to Kyle who was checking the hydraulic lines for any leaks.

"How's it look?"

Kyle gave him a nod. "I don't see any leaks and Captain Wilder says the pressure looks good. We're ready when Mitchell is, Mike."

"Thanks, Kyle. Be standing next to me at the rail when he goes in, we may need to pull him up if something happens with the hydraulics."

"Yeah, anything you need, boss." Kyle started to turn away, fear following him with every step he took.

"Wait a minute, Kyle." Mike stopped him before he could get too far away. Kyle turned and looked at him. Mike forgot just how young of a man he was, and what a first time on a crab boat this was turning out to be.

"You've done a hell of a job out here, kid. The best greenhorn I've seen in a long time out here. You've worked your ass off, never gave a single complaint, and always been someone we can count on. Even with this creature out here, you stood your ground and showed us what you're made of."

Kyle looked at him and shook his head. "I haven't done much, man. I'm scared as hell."

Mike smiled at him. "We're all scared, Kyle. But you're still out here working to give us a chance to get out of here. Justin, on the other hand, hasn't been dependable for anything other than getting drunk. You stepped up and became someone we can depend on."

Kyle's hands shook as he walked over to the railing in anticipation of his role of pulling Mitchell on board. He looked at Mike and asked him for a favor. "If I don't make it out of this, and you do Mike, will you give one of my belongings to my parents? That way they have something to bury and have some peace?"

"Hey, don't talk like that, Kyle. You're gonna make it through this, just like the rest of us are. We stick together and we'll be fine. Maybe the captain will have a change of heart about killing this thing once we get moving again."

John walked over to them. "It's time, guys."

They all looked at Mitchell, who started shaking uncontrollably again. "You got that ammo pouch on tight, John?" Mitchell asked.

John patted the pouch attached to his hip. "Don't worry, bud, she's on tight and ready to rock and roll."

Mitchell took one more gulp of fresh air and then put his goggles over his eyes and put his regulator in his mouth. Swinging his feet over the rail, he said a prayer to anyone that was listening and jumped feet first into the water.

******

Vibrations woke the sleeping monster; something had disturbed the natural rhythm of the ocean. Its eye opened wide as it scanned the surroundings, keeping still to not alert anything to its presence. The ocean was dark at these depths, but the vibrations painted a clear picture for the squid; prey was in the water.

******

As soon as Mitchell entered the cold water, he could feel that he was in a world that didn't belong to him. He scanned the water around him; the ocean was a murky combination of green and blue, visibility was almost nonexistent. The water appeared empty, but at the same time, it felt as if the creature could come out from anywhere. The mask that held tightly against his face made him begin to hyperventilate as he closed his eyes and tried to calm himself down.

Taking deep breaths, he slowly opened his eyes again, and looked around; still empty. Moving his arms, Mitchell began swimming to the rear of the ship and took the flashlight from his waistband. He flicked the button to the on position and shined the light to the propeller. It was exactly what the captain had said, the line from the pot was wrapped tightly around it.

Water suddenly moved behind him. He spun around, only to see open ocean as far as he could see. A current must have moved by him, he silently hoped to himself. He turned his attention back to the problem at hand and removed his knife from the sheath. This job was going to take longer than he thought, judging at how much rope was coiled.

But as Mitchell began cutting, he couldn't shake the feeling that he was being watched.

******

John looked out onto the ocean, hoping for a sign that Mitchell was going to be coming back up. He had already been in the water longer than he should have, but seeing no signs of distress, the cutting must be more extensive than they thought. Holding the rifle was starting to take a toll on his arms so John slung it over his shoulder and checked to make sure that the waist pouch containing the ammo was closed and secured on his belt.

Mike and Kyle were standing over the rail as well, staying close to the rope so they could pull Mitchell in quickly. The anticipation was showing clearly on their faces as they inspected every inch of the water, dreading anything happening to another one of their crewmates.

Suddenly, the ready room door opened, and Justin walked out, still slightly intoxicated but finally functional again. He walked to the rest of the crew and joined them in watching the water.

"How long's he been in?" Justin asked them.

"Too long, I don't know how much air he has in that tank, but he's got to be running low now," John answered.

Mike remarked in Mitchell's defense, "Give him some more time before we pull him back in, he'll get it done."

John rolled the rifle off his shoulder and held it out in a position to fire, index finger resting just above the trigger guard. "Let's hope so, Mike, I'm not counting him out but if he doesn't, we're screwed."

CHAPTER THIRTEEN:

After what had felt like an eternity, Mitchell was just about finished. He inspected his work and was satisfied he had gotten every piece of rope off. Shining the light along the propeller, he noticed something that he had never seen on the boat before. Thousands of small holes covered the metal underneath the boat, reminding him of a honeycomb from a beehive.

"How long has that been here?" he said to himself in his mask. For some reason, the marks looked familiar, like he had seen them before recently. As he stared longer, he realized the metal looked like it had been partially melted... by acid. Mitchell realized where he had seen this before; one of the pots they had brought up before being attacked by the squid had these same markings.

Panic flowed through his body again as he turned so he could start swimming for the surface, but his face was greeted by a giant eye staring back at him. Air bubbles shot out of his mask as he screamed and tried to swim away, but the tentacles belonging to the monster were too fast and strong. They held onto him tightly by all of his appendages, making him completely immobile and at the beast's whim.

Tears formed in Mitchell's eyes as he pleaded with the squid to let him go, his body shaking with fear as the giant eye simply stared at him. This monster knew nothing about remorse, and certainly nothing about the pleads of a sailor, begging for his life.

For several minutes, the squid simply held Mitchell in place, not hurting him but also not letting him go. The eye in its center started looking over his entire body, almost like it was studying him. After another minute, Mitchell stopped shaking as his curiosity overtook his fear. What was this creature waiting for? he wondered, feeling his body relax and his breathing becoming steady.

Without warning, the tentacles around his legs became tight, while the ones around his arms continued to feel loose. It was almost as if the squid was trying to feel his pulse through his wet suit. Mitchell looked at his belt and noticed his knife was still in its sheath. If he was quick, he might be able to slip his wrist out of its grasp and grab it.

Just as he was about to try to grab the knife, all the tentacles on him tightened. The beak opened wide, and a cloud of black liquid came spraying out. Mitchell was completely blinded by whatever the squid had expelled, complete darkness surrounded him. He started to panic again as he still felt the tightness of the squid holding onto him, but the creature still only held him there.

He looked up and saw a faint glimmer of the sun peeking through the black cloud, giving hope that at any second, John was going to begin firing the gun at the creature and he would be pulled to safety. But moments after that thought, Mitchell felt a severe burning sensation throughout his entire body.

******

"Hey, what's that?" John yelled to the rest of the crew, pointing down into the water.

Mike looked down over the rail and saw that the water at the side of the boat had turned black. It was so dark he couldn't see anything in the water.

"I don't know, you think we're leaking oil, John?" Mike answered.

"I don't think so, Mike, Wilder would have said something to me if we were. But I can't see shit in there."

Explanations ran through Mike's mind as he tried to think of a reason for what was in the water, but none made any sense. The only logical reason was an oil leak, but John was right, if that was the case, he would be in the engine room fixing it. But then it dawned on him exactly where the black cloud was.

"Oh shit!! Kyle, get over to the hydraulics and turn the block on!!" Mike yelled at the greenhorn.

John looked at Mike as he led the rifle into a shooting position. "What's going on? You see something, Mike?"

"That black stuff is right where Mitchell is!!"

******

Mitchell's body started to convulse, it felt like his skin was melting off his body.

What started as a feeling of a bad sunburn had turned into being dumped into a tank of boiling water. The dark cloud had started to fade away slightly and he brought his hands to his face; what he saw terrified him. What used to be a layer of white skin was now simply red muscle and tendons, he actually was melting away. He screamed in pain as the ocean around him blended into a combination of black and red, a twisted combination of blood and liquid from the squid.

The pain continued to grow more unbearable as each second went by. For some reason, the squid was unaffected by the substance. Mitchell remembered the slime that covered the boat from where the creature had touched, it was a protectant from its own acid.

The regulator in his mouth began to melt now, the rubber mouthpiece he bit down on had started melting to his lips, making his ability to breathe almost impossible. The plastic on the goggles and regulator had taken much longer to melt, protecting most of his face and eyes from the horrific pain his exposed body felt. Any second, Mike was going to pull him to safety and get him out of here.

But Mitchell watched helplessly as a smaller tentacle snaked its way through the water and placed the silver dollar-sized suction cups on his goggles and breathing respirator. He cried as he begged the squid not to do what he knew was going to happen next. The black eye simply stared at him as it ripped the protective pieces off his face.

The last thing he was able to see before he felt his eyes melt from his head was his lips that had been torn off his face, still attached to the mouthpiece. With the rest of his face now exposed, Mitchell screamed and cried violently as his face burned and melted into the sea, thrashing his body, making any attempt he could to try and free himself.

The more he tried to scream, the more the acidic liquid went into his body, eating away at his lungs and his esophagus. He began coughing and choking on water and bits of flesh that began coming from his throat.

Mitchell began to suddenly feel very tired as he felt the lifeforce leave his body. The pain had finally subsided, as the acid had eaten down past his nerve endings. As the liquid finished its work, the former boat diver was now no more than a skeleton with a couple of strands of flesh that finished sizzling away.

The squid thrust the bones into its beak, enjoying the marrow that remained in them and swallowed. It noticed something in the water, a long, eel-looking creature that had been attached to its prey. Moving closer and inspecting it, the squid determined that this strange creature posed no threat. Reaching one of its tentacles up, it snaked the suction cups around it and pulled.

******

"Pull him up now!!" Mike screamed, running for the hydraulic controls to get his crew member out of the water.

The safety line suddenly tightened, and the boat started to roll to the side, causing all the gear and the crew to slide towards the railing. John nearly dropped the rifle as he held on as tight as he could, preparing to see tentacles at any second. Mike got back on his feet and made his way to the control panel while Kyle began pulling on the line with all his might.

Arriving at the control panel, Mike pushed the button to activate the block, but was greeted with the sight of a hydraulic hose spraying hydraulic fluid all over the deck. No matter how many times he pushed the button, the block refused to begin turning. The boat continued to roll to its side, creating the panic that the boat would roll completely over.

Mike ran to the intercom. "The block won't work, we got a hydraulic leak, and it won't turn on!!"

"Forget the block and cut that rope! That thing's gonna pull the boat over!" Captain Wilder's voice yelled from the intercom.

"But Mitchell's still down there!"

"If you don't cut that rope, we're gonna be joining him down there. Cut the damn rope, Mike, we don't have a choice." For a shocking change, Mike heard a tone of remorse as the captain gave the order to cut Mitchell's only way to safety.

Mike made his way to the end of the safety line and pulled his work knife out and began cutting. Mike yelled at Kyle to let go of the rope.

"Why are you cutting the rope!?" Kyle yelled in confusion. "We need to get him out of there!"

Mike got angry as he kept cutting the thick rope. "If we don't cut him off that thing's gonna pull the boat over. If it's pulling on the rope, then that means it has Mitchell in its tentacles."

Kyle let go of the rope and tried to steady himself as the boat continued to roll.

With each strand that was cut, he cursed himself for what he was doing. Another friend was dying on his watch, and this time, he was the one sending him to his doom. But he had no choice.

The last thread to the rope was cut and the boat sprung back from the release of the massive weight. The crew again were knocked to their feet as the boat leveled out and teetered back and forth. Justin was the first one to his feet as he started making a run for the ready room but was knocked on his back as a tentacle as big around as a small tree swung into his chest.

"Oh shit, it's here!" Justin yelled and coughed as he tried to regain his breath, the wind knocked out of him from the force of his fall.

John stood up and watched the red tentacle swim through the air as if it was searching for its next victim. He brought the rifle scope up to his eye and followed the large mass with the crosshairs. Left, right, diagonal, the tentacle moved with cheetah-like speed, making it almost impossible for John to get a clear shot.

He ran closer to the squid's tentacle as he realized it was thicker around the bottom and would provide an easier shot. Bringing the rifle back up again, his scope was filled with red and he squeezed the trigger.

Boom!

Blue-tinted blood erupted from the center of the tentacle as the bullet ripped through its flesh. The squid flinched as the pain coursed through its nerve endings. John walked closer as he fired round after round into the creature until finally, he heard a click instead of a boom. The gun was empty.

John opened the bolt again and unzipped the ammo pouch and started putting bullets into the gun. He got three loaded into the rifle before a second tentacle burst through the surface of the water and swept his legs out from under him. As John hit the deck, the brass cartridges flew out of the pouch. The second tentacle held in the air another moment before swinging down, attempting to crush the engineer. John rolled out of the way just in time as the appendage landed right where he was just lying, leaving broken deck boards in its aftermath.

He closed the bolt on the rifle and slung it over his shoulder as he tried to pick up the fallen bullets. A third tentacle gripped onto the railing and started to pull the boat over again. He was knocked to his feet again and rolled onto his stomach. He looked over to see the bullets rolling to the edge of the railing.

John crawled as fast as he could to try and stop them. "No, no, no!!" he yelled as the remaining bullets rolled underneath the water opening at the rail and fell into the sea.

"Fuck!" he screamed as he slammed his fist onto the deck boards. He didn't think it could get any worse until he looked over and saw Kyle being picked up by the second tentacle.

"Someone help!! It's got me!" he yelled at the top of his lungs.

John took a breath to steady his hands as he put the crosshairs on the tentacle and fired another shot. Boom! The tentacle jerked as the bullet tore through the flesh and dropped the greenhorn back onto the deck.

Kyle got to his feet and ran as fast as he could out of harm's way, running into Mike who was picking Justin up from the deck.

"Everyone back inside now!" Mike screamed as he grabbed ahold of Justin and pushed him towards the door. He dodged a sweeping tentacle as he ran to the intercom to alert the captain. "Go, go, go!! Get us out of here!"

The boat slowly lurched forward as Captain Wilder increased the throttle as fast as it would go. He steered the boat left to try and put some distance between themselves and the beast. But the squid was using its suction cups to hold onto the bottom of the boat and continued its attack.

Mike saw John standing in the middle of the deck with the rifle in his hand, but for some reason wasn't firing it. "Shoot that thing, John! We gotta get it off the boat!" he yelled.

"We only have two bullets left for it, Mike!" John yelled back at him.

"You shot all those bullets already?"

John shook his head in embarrassment as he tried to explain as quickly as possible what had happened. "That damn thing knocked me down and the bullets fell out of the pouch and rolled through the rail. I've got two rounds left in the gun."

"We need to think of something fast, that thing's gonna pull the boat over again if we don't do something," Mike replied.

An idea formed in his head, something so crazy it just might work. "Keep that thing occupied, I'll be right back." He ran to the engine room to get some supplies.

John yelled back at him, "How the hell am I supposed to do that?"

"I don't know, try anything. Just don't get eaten." And he disappeared into the engine room.

******

Captain Wilder couldn't believe how strong this thing was, almost pulling the boat completely over more than once so far. He pushed the one engine they had as hard as it would go. While he was happy to have an engine again, the weight of the creature was bogging the boat down badly. He looked at the speedometer: six miles an hour. At this rate they wouldn't be able to outrun a flock of birds with how slow they were going, let alone this sea monster. He grabbed the microphone and gave another order, "You guys better do something quick or that thing's gonna tear this boat apart." As soon as the words left his mouth, one of the smaller tentacles reared back and whipped into the side window of the wheelhouse, shattering the glass as it slithered inside.

He ducked just in the nick of time as the tentacle whipped across the room, missing his head by a matter of inches. Looking up, he saw his Victorinox knife sitting in the cupholder next to the throttle. He grabbed the "Vicky", and quickly inspected the small 4-inch blade in his hand; it would have to do.

The squid's tentacle came back around and grabbed onto the captain's left arm and tried to pull him through the small window it had come from. Using all his might, Wilder plunged the knife down to the handle into the flesh, causing it to release its grasp from him. Anger flowed through his veins as he lunged at the creature that was destroying his boat and began stabbing as many times as he could. Blue blood sprayed across the small room as Captain Wilder went into a blood fury.

The tentacle tried to retreat out the window but Wilder grabbed onto it and braced himself onto the floor. Pulling the knife out, he stabbed the top of the tentacle and began sawing it as fast as he could, hoping to cut it in half. But as he started sawing, the knife broke in half as the tentacle jerked; he looked around for something else to aid him in his efforts.

His eyes fell upon his emergency survival box that was sitting under the boat's control dash. His mind quickly raced through what was in the contents of the box and he smiled when he remembered what was in it: flares.

He extended his arm to try and reach the box while he held onto the squid with the other; the squid tentacle was becoming more violent and erratic, trying with all its might to escape being on the wrong side of the fight. Tom struggled as sweat ran down his head from the strain of holding onto the monster. He could feel the appendage begin to slip out of his arm.

"Ohhh no you don't, you son of a bitch. You're not going anywhere," he sneered as he used every last ounce of strength to reach out and grab onto the box, pulling it to him. With one hand he popped the cover open and grabbed exactly what he needed, a high temperature road flare.

Wilder wrapped his legs around the tentacle to keep it from escaping as he took the cap off the flare and grinned as he eyed the hole in the squid that he had made with the "Vicky" knife. He struck the top of the flare with the top cover and a two-inch flame erupted out the top.

Captain Wilder grinned wider and yelled, "I hope this hurts, you prick!!" He shoved the flare into the open wound.

The tentacle thrashed violently as its flesh was seared by the 2,000 degree flame that began cooking it from the inside. Smoke filled the room along with the smell of burnt squid. Wilder gave out a savage laugh as he relished at the pain being caused to the creature, savoring every second.

Finally, exhaustion plagued the salty captain as the adrenaline was no longer enough to help him keep ahold of the monster. His grip gave way as the tentacle slipped from his legs and disappeared back through the window.

He lay on the floor, trying to regain his strength to stand back up. While he waited, a thought came across his mind. He had just had a one-on-one fight with this thing and won, with nothing but a knife and a road flare. Grabbing onto the counter, he pulled himself up and plopped back down in his seat. This thing may be big, he thought, but it could be killed.

******

John was running out of options to try and keep the squid distracted and was running out of chances to not become food for it. Twice already he had narrowly avoided the fast-moving tentacles that seemed to have minds of their own. He still had the rifle with him, but it might as well have been a cap gun since he only had two bullets left, which he knew wouldn't be enough to stop the giant squid.

A tentacle slithered behind and grabbed ahold of John by his waist, beginning to lift him up into the air. He punched and kicked as hard as he could, but he was no match for the super predator. He turned his head and saw where the creature was taking him: towards the water.

Just as John thought this was his last few seconds of living, Mike came running from the ready room, holding what looked like a flaming bottle in his hand.

"Mike, help!!" John screamed as he saw he was running out of deck boards under his feet.

Mike ran as fast as he could with the homemade fire bomb and threw it at the tentacle that had ahold of his friend. The bottle burst into flames as it covered the flesh of the squid's tentacle and began charring the flesh to black.

The squid released its grip on the engineer as it tried to shake the burning flames off of it but proved to be useless as the flames stuck to the flesh and continued to burn. John fell to the floor as Mike came over and helped him up with his hand.

"What the hell was that?" John yelled to him, and he took his hand.

"Oh, just a little drink I cooked up for it with some flammable liquids we had in the engine room. Added a little plastic to it too to make it sticky," Mike chuckled.

"Well, it looks like it's working, that thing's still cooking. Let's get out of here, Mike!" John remarked.

The tentacle continued to shake violently as the liquid continued to sear its flesh, bits of flaming plastic beginning to rain down onto the deck. Finally, like the snap of a finger, the tentacles disappeared back into the water. The boat began to pick up speed as they could feel the weight of the squid release from the bottom of the boat. For now, it was gone.

Mike looked up at the wheelhouse and noticed the broken window on the side. "Let's go and check on the captain. With any luck, that thing did us a favor and ate him."

"One could only hope," John remarked as he limped to the door, feeling a sprain in his leg from the fall.

CHAPTER FOURTEEN:

The remainder of the crew sat at the galley table in the safety of the boat, each of them nursing their wounds from the battle with the squid. John had an ice pack on his lower back from falling, Captain Wilder was busy cleaning the slime off of him, and Mike tried to push the thoughts of what happened to Mitchell out of his mind. Justin and Kyle had been spared any injuries other than a few bruises.

Justin went over to the counter and started pouring cups of coffee for everyone; it wasn't fresh, but at this point no one was going to complain. Smoke from cigarettes and the smell of old coffee lingered in the air as everyone told their stories of what had happened to them. The men on deck were even impressed with the captain's one on one fight with one of the tentacles.

John was the last to share his story as he tried to leave out the part where he lost all but two bullets for the gun.

"Well, at least you managed to keep hold of that rifle even after it picked ya up, John. We still got a chance to kill that thing as long as we have that," Captain Wilder said as he pointed at the bolt action rifle.

John gave him a nervous laugh. "Uh, yeah. There's a small little detail I left out in my story, Cap."

Wilder was nursing his arm while he laughed. "Like what? You crapped your pants when it picked you up? Hahahaha."

"Uh, no. I... uh... dropped the bullets and they went under the rail."

"What!" Captain Wilder yelled. "How many did you drop!?"

John was silent for several moments before he dropped what knew was going to be a devastating blow. "All of them..."

"Fuck!" Tom stood up and removed his ball cap off of his head, pulling on his hair. "Are there even any bullets left in the gun?!"

"We have two rounds left in it," John answered. Mike cringed at the number.

Justin plopped his face into his hands and started to cry. "We're screwed, we're not gonna get out of here."

Captain Wilder paced around the table with his hands on the back of his head, his face red from frustration. "For once, I think I agree with Justin." He pointed back at the rifle sitting on the table. "That thing was our only chance to kill that thing out there and make some money. But thanks to John, we might as well throw it over the rail."

"It wasn't his fault, Tom," Mike interjected. "That thing pulled on the boat when he was reloading, and they spilled out. It would have happened to any of us if we had the rifle."

"Well, I'm out of ideas." Captain Wilder walked over to the counter top in another angry rage and swiped everything off of it. He suddenly screamed out, "Owww, what the hell was that?!"

He brought his hand up to his face and saw a small hook stuck in the side. "Oh, great. Just what I need right now, can someone hand me a pair of cutters?"

John grabbed a pair of wire cutters off the adjacent counter and handed them to him. Wilder pushed the hook through the rest of the skin until the point and barb poked out and cut the end off with the cutters. As he pulled the rest of the hook out of his hand, Mike stared in a trance at the hook as a small amount of blood spilled onto the floor.

"Hey, at least it was just one hook, Cap. I knew a guy that stuck his hand in a tackle box, and he pulled it out covered in treble hooks," Justin said, trying to lighten the mood.

Mike stroked his chin as he kept thinking. "Do we still have those hooks from Marlin fishing this summer?"

Captain Wilder started bandaging his hand as he got a bottle and a syringe from the first aid box to prevent any chance of tetanus from the hook. "We shouldn't, Kyle and Justin were supposed to have all that stuff taken off before we left for this trip." He jabbed the needle into his leg and administered the medicine.

Kyle reluctantly spoke up to address the issue. "Uh, they're still on board, guys. I never got the chance to take them off, Justin and I got pretty busy trying to get all the extra bait loaded up on the boat."

"Well what the hell, guys? Why didn't you say anything before..."

John cut the captain off before he could finish, "What are you thinking, Mike?"

Mike started pacing the galley. "We have Marlin hooks, and we still have some pots left... what if we made a trap for this thing?"

"What kind of a trap?" Wilder asked, clearly intrigued by the idea.

Mike stood up and grabbed a piece of paper and a pen off of the counter and sat back down. He drew a crude picture of one of their crab pots as he explained his idea. The rest of the crew stood around as the drawing unfolded.

"We take one of our pots, and we cover the thing with as many hooks as we have, using the strongest fishing line we have on the boat to attach them. Then we cram as much bait as we can into it to help lure the creature to it. With some luck, it'll attack the trap and get caught in the hooks. With all the hooks that are covering it, the more it fights to get away, the more ensnared it'll be." Mike put the pen down as he finished the drawing, revealing a crab pot that looked like it had come out of Hell itself.

The engineer took the picture off the table and inspected the design. "This could work, Mike, but there's a few problems with it. As soon as we put this thing in the ocean, it's gonna sink to the bottom with all the weight. And even if it attacks the trap, we don't have line that will hold it there indefinitely. Soon after it gets snagged, it'll break the lines and get away, and it's gonna be pissed."

"Then we kill it while it's trapped," Captain Wilder announced.

Justin chuckled and shook his head. "And how do we do that? Like you said, that rifle was our best chance and it's not like we're a war ship, we're a crab boat." He lit a cigarette as he sat back down at the table.

Mike stared at the flame from the lighter and another idea popped into his head. "That thing reacts to fire, maybe we can burn it enough to kill it."

Captain Wilder shook his head. "That's gonna be almost impossible with it being in the water, we don't have the spare fuel anyways to do something like that. There has to be another way of killing it."

Everyone thought of what they could do to kill a squid that was almost as big as their boat. The perfect plan that Mike had thought of was quickly turning into a fool's idea.

"The acetylene bottles!!" John cried out.

"What?" Kyle asked.

"We have bottles and bottles of acetylene for the welder in the engine room, big ones. That stuff's highly flammable, we can stuff them into the pot and if we can get them to explode, that should be enough to kill it."

Justin again raised doubts about the plan. "How are we supposed to make the bottles explode if the trap is at the bottom of the ocean?"

Kyle had an idea. "We have spare buoys, don't we? They float, we can string all the spares on the outside of the trap and that should be enough to keep it on the surface. Then we just find a way to explode the bottles."

John picked up the rifle. "We still have two bullets for this, we can shoot one of the bottles and then use fire somehow to ignite the rest of them."

"We have a flare gun and some flares from the emergency kit we can use," Captain Wilder spoke. "We get the pot launched into the water, get a safe distance, wait until the squid's trapped, and then shoot the tanks. I think this could work, guys."

"I'm sure it's not going to be as simple as it sounds. There's a lot that can go wrong, what if the squid doesn't go after the bait?" Justin asked.

Mike gave his thoughts on the matter, "I'm no expert, but I'd say with how scarce animals are out here it's not gonna pass up on a free meal. I think this squid's eaten all of the animals in the area and now it's desperate for food. That would explain why it risked coming onto the boat and eating all the crab in our hold. It's starving."

"How do you know that thing is what happened to the crab?" Kyle asked.

"There was slime all over the cover, just like what's been on everything since we encountered it when it took Travis. It came aboard to feed because there's no other food. And now it wants us," Mike said gravely.

Captain Wilder slammed his uninjured fist onto the table, shaking the cups off of it. "Well, he's got something else he can eat on. Come on, guys, we've got a lot of work to do. Get some coffee going 'cause the sun's going down; we're gonna have to work through the night to get this thing built."

"Great, another long shift," Justin remarked as he rubbed his eyes, putting fresh coffee grounds into the coffee pot.

The rest of the crew went to different areas of the boat and began working on the most important project of their lives, with the faint hope that their efforts would be enough for them to kill this demon of the sea.

******

The squid nursed its injured limbs, coating them in excess slime that it had secreted to aid in healing. Not only had it underestimated the prey floating on the water, but also the creatures that dwelled inside of it. While the fight was not a total loss, thanks to the small meal it got to enjoy, it had still come at a price. Instead of attacking, the squid knew it would need to rest, allowing the slime to do its work on the burns it had sustained.

Morning would be a different story, the time for stalking was over. It would use all of the remaining energy it had to deal a final devastating blow to its prey, allowing the squid to feast on the flesh at its leisure. Once every ounce of meat was consumed, the squid would move to different waters, continuing its domination of the ocean.

The large eye slowly closed as sleep took hold, allowing its body to move with the current. The tentacles gently swayed back and forth to keep pace with the creature above, allowing it to swim while it slept. This used valuable energy, but was a small sacrifice compared to trying to find the prey after a night of travel. A perk to being such a terror of the ocean was that there was no need to fear while it slept. And sleep the creature did.

CHAPTER FIFTEEN:

The men had worked tirelessly throughout the night, all of them had pushed their capacity for exhaustion to their limits. Six pots of coffee and multiple packs of cigarettes later, their creation was finally born. The metal pot sat on the deck, over twenty bottles of the flammable gas were sitting inside along with buoys and over four hundred 7 inch steel fishing hooks. The last item to be added was what was going to lure the beast in, the last of their remaining cod fish.

Justin and Kyle had spent hours putting the rest of the ship's frozen bait into the bait chopper and then scooping the mixture into bait bags. To help entice the squid to attack the pot, they added any fresh food they could that contained a strong smell, from whole frozen chickens to Harvey's collection of sardines that he used to enjoy.

As the sun began breaking over the horizon, Mike and John closed the gate to the pot and tied it off as tight as they could. The crew stood around the trap and relished what they had made.

Captain Wilder lit the last cigarette in his pack and flicked the empty container over the side. "We did it. Now all we have to worry about is that thing taking the bait."

"That shouldn't be a problem," Kyle said as he covered his nose. "This thing smells like a sewer pipe."

Mike nodded his head. "Good, that'll help bring it in. Now, everyone knows their positions, right?"

The crew nodded and went over the plan one last time.

Captain Wilder spoke first, "I'll be up in the wheelhouse per usual. I'll keep the boat slow and once the pot's in the water, I'll get us a safe distance away from it so John can shoot it with the rifle."

Next up was Kyle, "I'll be standing by with the flare gun and when I get the word from John, I'll shoot the tanks with it."

"I'll be on standby, waiting for anyone that needs some kelp," Justin said, as he took a small drag from his flask in his pocket.

John looked at him with glaring eyes. "Really? The time we need you sober the most, you're drinking?"

Justin put the cap on the flask and put it in his back pocket. "Hey, I'm nervous, cut me some slack. If this plan actually works, then I'll give up drinking when we get back." He wiped his mouth and steadied himself as the boat gently rocked.

"Back to what we were discussing," Mike interjected. "I'll be at the hydraulic controls to drop the pot in the water. You got the hydraulic line fixed, right, John?"

"Yes sir, luckily it wasn't too bad of a fix. We must of had too much pressure and blew the line. But I swapped it with a new one and gave it a test, we shouldn't have any issues with it," John boasted.

"Ok, good. Well guys, this is it. Good luck to all of you; with some luck we may just pull this off. Now it's time to get to our positions," Mike ordered.

The crew started to move about the deck when the greenhorn asked a harrowing question that brought the whole deck silent.

"What if this doesn't work?"

They looked at each other and didn't know what to say to him, afraid to desert any hope that the young kid had left.

Mike finally broke the silence, "Then God help us."

******

The nerve endings on the squid's tentacles began firing impulses to its brain; there was a change in the prey. Through the night it had kept a consistent speed, but now it had slowed to an almost stop. It must be getting ready to make an attack. The squid stirred and began swimming in circles below the monster above, allowing the blood to flow through its tentacles and body.

It brought its crippled tentacle to its eye. While it had healed significantly while it slept, anger flowed through the squid once more. It recalled the battle from the previous day and would not make the same mistakes. This time, it would finish the creature off once and for all.

******

Mike stood at the controls and activated the crane. While he had been running the crane for over a decade, it was one of the hardest jobs on the boat. One wrong adjustment at the controls and it could send the pot swinging around the deck, and into anyone that stood there. After giving the controls a quick test and satisfied that it was functioning correctly, he told John to check the knot on the top of the pot.

"Make sure that knot is gonna hold, John!" Mike yelled to him. "It's gonna have to stay tied while I lift the pot over the railing!"

"You got it, boss!" John answered.

Mike watched him carefully weave thick rope around one of the metal bars of the pot and tie a sophisticated knot, giving it a hard tug to make sure it was secured. Once he was done, John turned and gave Mike a thumbs up, and went to his position by the rail.

Mike went to the speaker at the bait station and relayed his status to the captain. "We're all good on our end, Cap. Just let us know when we can set the trap."

The voice that came across the speaker was cold and void of any human emotion. "Set it."

Mike hurried back to the controls and gave one final look at all the men around him. Kyle and John stood at the rail, their faces made of stone as he gave them the nod: it was time. He looked towards the ready room and saw Justin, who was taking another pull from his flask. The boat rocked and Justin had to catch himself on the door handle to stop himself from falling over, more from the whiskey than from the boat.

Mike shook his head as he turned his attention back to the controls. He moved the levers and began to raise the pot above the deck. The pot gently swayed back and forth as it rose just high enough to be able to clear the railing. Mike started to move the pot towards the railing when he saw Justin stumbling towards him.

"Justin! What are you doing?" he yelled, bringing the pot trap to a stop.

Justin kept stumbling towards him, holding his flask out in his hand. "Hey Mike, you look a little on edge! I figured you could use a little drink to calm your nerves!" A drunken smile broke across his face as he made it half way across the deck, directly next to the hanging crab pot.

******

The squid swam as fast as it could as it rose toward its prey. Swimming in a circular pattern, it built as much momentum as possible. As it came around its last turn, it saw the side of the creature, and used all of its energy as it rammed into its side.

******

The words barely left Mike's lips as he tried to tell Justin to go back when the boat was rocked by the force of what felt like an oncoming train. The whole boat pitched to the side as the squid hit the right side of the boat. John and Kyle held on to the rail with all their might to stop them from being thrown onto the ground. Justin, however, was not so lucky.

He made it one more step before the overhanging pot swung into the side of his body. Mike watched in horror as the two-thousand-pound trap smashed into Justin's body. He heard the snapping of his ribs as Justin let out a high pitched scream that shook Mike to his core. The hooks attached to the pot grabbed ahold of his flesh and swung his body like a pendulum, infusing him into the trap.

The flask from his hand fell to the deck and glided under the railing as the boat steadied itself. Justin continued to scream as he begged the crew to get him out, thrashing his body in an attempt to escape, but only succeeding in ensnaring himself more.

"Mike, get me out of this thing!" Justin cried. The hooks had been buried as far in as they could go, blood seeping onto the deck boards and running under the rail.

Mike yelled to the two crewmates, "Help get him out of there, guys! Pull him off NOW!!"

Kyle and John ran to the aid of Justin and began trying to pull him off of the hooks. Justin screamed out as his flesh began tearing from the embedded hooks covering his body, but his body refused to leave. John looked over at Mike and gave him a grim shake of his head. He ran to the deck boss and lowered his voice.

"It's no use, Mike, those hooks are in him almost all the way to the top. We're gonna have to lower the pot and cut each of the lines one by one, then hope that he doesn't die from infection until we can get him to a hospital. And he's lost a lot of blood already."

Mike looked at Justin and saw his face was turning extremely pale, the liquor he had been drinking wasn't doing him any favors as it was thinning his blood and causing him to bleed faster than normal. Justin tried to extend a hand to Mike but stopped after several inches as the line from the hook embedded in it went taut, jostling him with more pain.

"Please..." Justin sobbed. "I can't take much more of this, Mike..."

Turning for the bait station, Mike ran to the speaker and informed the captain of what had happened.

"Justin's stuck to the pot, Tom, we can't pull him off. We're gonna have to set it down and cut him out of it," Mike relayed to him.

Captain Wilder's voice was cold as ice, "We don't have time for that, dump the pot in the ocean."

Mike looked up at the wheelhouse in shock. "What about Justin?"

Laughter came across the speaker. "Looks like we got some live bait for the trap, Mike."

"You know I can't do that, Tom. I'm not gonna send him to be eaten by that thing," Mike answered. "We can get him out, we just need some time."

"Time is something we don't have, you think what rocked the boat was simply a rogue wave?" Captain Wilder asked him. "That squid's attacking already, we have to get that trap in the water now. It's his own fault for being a drunken idiot, Mike, and now he's gonna pay the consequence. You have to make a hard decision, welcome to the crabbing industry. Kill him, or kill all of us, your choice."

Mike said a prayer for his soul as he walked back to his position at the hydraulic controls. He yelled at Kyle and John to return to their positions at the railing. They looked at him in shock and disbelief.

"You heard me, get back to the rail now!!" Mike hid the pain in his voice just barely. The two men ran back to their positions, not daring to say a word. Justin looked over to Mike and couldn't understand what was happening.

"What are you telling them that for?" he asked weakly. "You're getting me out of this, right?"

Mike looked down at the floor as he activated the controls and began raising the pot up more, and slowly moved it towards the rail.

"Wait.. No.. Nooo!!" Justin yelled as loud as he could, crying and sobbing as he thrashed around in a frenzy. "You can't do this to me, Mike! I'm still attached to the trap! PLEASE!!"

Mike felt like he was going to throw up, he was sending another man to their death, and he couldn't do anything about it. "I'm sorry, Justin.. I'm... I'm sorry."

Once the pot was dangling over the water, Mike lowered it into the water and slipped the crane hook out from it.

The trap was now set.

******

A large vibration shook through the water, alerting the squid that something had entered its domain. Before it could investigate the disturbance, it started to taste blood coming in through its beak. Whatever had come into the water was large and injured. The sensors on the end of the tentacles detected smaller vibrations rippling through the water, the telltale sign of something struggling.

While the squid would have preferred to use caution, the taste of blood mixed with the growing hunger drove it into a frenzy of bloodlust and anger. It whipped its tentacles behind it to give it a boost of speed as it darted straight above at the black shadow sitting above the surface.

******

Kyle tried to cover his ears as the screams from Justin rang through the sea, sending shivers down his spine. The flare gun shook in his hands as the boat pulled into position, roughly fifty meters away from the trap.

"Is this gonna be far enough away from the explosion?" Kyle asked John.

John shrugged his shoulders. "I don't really know honestly, that's a lot of bottles of gas sitting in that trap. We're not gonna know for sure until it goes off, if I had to guess though I'd say it may be a little too much."

Captain Wilder's voice shouted over the deck speakers, "Any sign of it yet?"

Mike shook his head at him. Other than the hit that had forced Justin into the trap, the creature was gone. "Keep an eye out, John, it can't be too far away! We need to be ready for when it..."

Suddenly, the water around the crab pot exploded in a shower of water and tentacles. Kyle and John froze in terror and amazement as the squid attacked the pot with more ferocity than they had ever seen before. Suction-cupped limbs latched onto the hook-covered pot, attempting to reach the bloody food inside.

The hooks embedded into its flesh, ensnaring the monster and driving it into a painfilled rage. The squid thrashed and attacked wildly, unaware of what exactly was attacking it, but feeling the pain of a thousand cuts all over its body. It tried to escape by retreating back to the depths, but its tentacles and body were ensnared to the food it was trying to consume. The big eye looked at what was causing the pain and realized what had happened.

What it had thought was food was actually one of the traps the humas used for catching the small crustations and had somehow turned it into a trap for itself. The squid scanned around and could see the humas not far away, and realized the animal it had been hunting was something used to carry the humans. Pain fired all across its body and tentacles, sending the squid into a fury. It whipped and attacked the pot to try and escape, but it was firmly snagged.

John looked out from the railing and raised his fist high in the air. "We got it, it's snagged, Mike! That thing's pissed too, I don't think that trap's gonna hold long."

Mike ran beside him and watched the carnage ensue as the creature tried to destroy the pot. "You better shoot one of those bottles quick, John, this may be our only chance. Kyle, get ready with that flare gun!"

Kyle loaded one of the flares into the handheld flare gun and extended his arm out to aim. As he did, he noticed Justin still caught in the middle of the chaos, and one of the tentacles sensed him. "Oh no, guys, that thing's noticed Justin."

CHAPTER SIXTEEN:

Justin, still conscious, screamed louder than he ever had before at the terrifying sight before him. He was completely surrounded by the monster and had no hope of escaping. One of the tentacles slithered to him and wrapped around his waist, pulling his body from the trap.

"Ahhh, no!! Somebody do something!!" Justin screamed as he felt the hooks tearing the flesh on his body. He felt like he was being pulled apart in a thousand different directions.

John brought the rifle scope to his eye and saw the carnage as if he was standing right next to the beast. He could see blood pouring from where the hooks were embedded as the squid pulled harder after meeting the resistance of the thick fishing line. With one final jerk, it had ripped Justin off of the hooks. John began throwing up as he saw pieces of his flesh fly through the air and heard a scream that reminded John of a wild animal being skinned alive.

A second tentacle swam through the air and began coiling around the young deckhand's head, slowly beginning to squeeze.

He spat blood out of his mouth as he begged for his life, feeling the pressure in his head building. "Please... Stop..."

The tentacle gave one final squeeze and Justin's head burst, sending gray brain matter and blood flying through the air. The squid pulled his limp body down below the water and quickly feasted on its meal.

Mike watched the entire event unfold, and he became sick to his stomach. He dropped to one knee as he covered his eyes with his hand; another man he had known for years had died because of what he had to do. No matter the flaws the younger deckhand had, he didn't deserve to die like this.

"Shoot one of those damn bottles, John, so we can kill this thing!" Mike yelled at him.

John tried to steady himself as he aimed the rifle. "I'm trying, Mike, but it's not as easy as it looks. That thing is moving all over the place and I can't get a clear shot!"

All he could see through the scope lens was a mixture of ocean and squid, intermixing together. John knew their time was running short as he caught a glimpse of one of the tentacles curling around the edge of the pot and tried to pull it apart.

"Come on... Come on, you bastard, stay still for me..." John whispered to himself as he slowed down his breathing, preparing to take a shot. For a brief second, the tentacles parted, and John got a clear view of one of the bottles. He began squeezing the trigger.

"Goodnight, sweetie," John grinned.

"SHOOT THE DAMN RIFLE!!" Captain Widler yelled over the speaker.

Startled, John jerked the rifle as he pulled the trigger.

BANG!

The shot missed.

He looked up at the wheelhouse and yelled at the captain, "What the hell was that? I had a perfect shot, and you chose right then to start screaming?!"

"Come on, John, shoot again! It's breaking free!" Mike yelled.

John worked the bolt on the rifle and loaded their last round into the chamber. He brought it back to his eye and could see the pot was starting to come apart: this was their last chance. "Be ready with that flare gun, kid."

After several seconds, the squid tried to submerge into the ocean again, and gave a full view of every bottle in the pot. He took a breath and slowly let it out as he squeezed the trigger one final time.

BANG!

John looked through the scope and saw gas releasing from one of the bottles; he had hit his target. "Now Kyle, shoot it with the flare! The gas is leaking!"

Kyle closed one eye and fired the flare gun at the trap. It shot and landed fifteen feet short. He cursed and loaded another flare into the gun and aimed.

"Hurry, before all the gas escapes!" Mike yelled to him.

Kyle raised his aim higher and pulled the trigger, but nothing happened. He smacked the gun in his hand but no matter how many times he tried, the flare gun wouldn't fire again.

"This thing's broken, it won't shoot now. What do we do?" Kyle asked, trying not to panic. He could see the squid was just about free and knew the next place it would be going was straight at them.

John looked and saw the squid had finally broken the crab pot apart, hooks and parts of the trap still clung to its body. But now it was able to move about freely and it turned to face the side of the boat. He ran to the wheelhouse speaker. "We need to get out of here, Wilder, it's free, its gonna come right at us!"

No answer came back from the speaker.

"Where the hell did he go?" John yelled to Mike. "We need to get out of here. Look, it's headed this way!"

All three crew members looked out and saw the squid swimming along the surface of the water, swimming right at them. Mike was about to turn away when he noticed several bottles of acetylene following it, held on by hooks and part of the pot webbing. He looked on deck to see if there was anything they could use to kill it and saw several barrels of fuel they kept on board.

"I've got an idea! Help me get that barrel over here, guys!" Mike ordered them as he ran to the fuel. John and Kyle followed close behind and turned it on its side. Grabbing a hatchet from the bait station, he told them to roll it to the railing where the cutout was for the water to go back to the ocean.

Kyle started rolling the barrel. "What are we doing all this for?"

John laughed as he helped them roll. "'Cause we're gonna burn this bastard to death. This fuel will sit on the surface right where it's swimming and light him on fire. Good thinking, Mike!"

"Will this be enough to kill it?"

Mike shrugged as he panted from exhaustion. " I hope so, man. If not, I'll make a run for the controls and get us out of here."

They made it to the rail and Mike began hitting the barrel with the hatchet until a fist-sized hole formed at the bottom of the lid. Amber-colored liquid poured out and funneled through the cutout and into the ocean. After several minutes, the fuel barrel was empty.

John helped Kyle throw the barrel over the side. "Perfect, now all we need is some way to light it... Hey, where'd it go?"

Mike and Kyle looked up over the rail and realized John was right, the squid was gone. They scanned the water on both sides of the boat and saw no sign of it.

John walked over to Kyle and took the flare gun from him and inspected it, quickly realizing what the problem was. "Here's what's wrong, man, the flare's a dud. That's why it wouldn't fire."

He loaded a new flare into it and handed it back to the greenhorn. "You're all good to go now, bud."

The boat rocked as tentacles came over the railing, pulling on the metal, almost flipping it completely over. The flare gun flew out of Kyle's hand and went over the railing, falling into the ocean. Their only chance was gone.

Mike looked to the side and was horrified by what he saw; the squid was trying to climb onto the boat. Grabbing a hold of his hatchet, he ran to the closest tentacle and began hacking at it. "Come on, we got to get it off the boat, it's gonna pull us over!"

John and Kyle grabbed a knife and began cutting every tentacle they could. Blood covered the deck boards and the crew. A tentacle raced across the deck and knocked Kyle's legs out from under him and coiled around his waist. Before it could carry him away, Mike ran and jumped on top of it; he wasn't going to let another person die on his watch. He swung the axe over and over again until the foot diameter appendage was severed.

Mike pried the suction cups off of him and helped him to his feet as he saw John cutting a tentacle that was trying to wrap around one of his legs. They ran to his aid and helped cut and chop the tentacle until it released him and went back over the railing, leaving a blood trail in its aftermath.

But as one tentacle left, three more took its place. They looked at the oncoming carnage and realized that there wasn't much more they could do.

"Mike... I don't think we're gonna make it out of this," John admitted as they backed away towards the other side of the boat.

More of the squid was seen as the boat rolled from the immense weight of its body. With one more pull, the eye of the beast rose above the railing, and saw its prey. Now it would savor the last of the prey it had pursued. It raised its appendage and prepared to scoop all three in final motion.

"Hey baby, look what I got for ya!!"

The deckhand looked up at the voice and saw Captain Wilder standing on the roof of the wheelhouse, holding something in his hands. The squid turned its attention to the new threat and attempted to swipe it away, but the human had ducked out of the way just in time.

"What's in his hands?" John asked.

Mike's jaw dropped as he added up what he saw. "Hand flares."

Captain Wilder smiled as he ignited the flares. "Looks like I win." He ran and jumped off of the roof, and right into the fuel-soaked water.

The flares ignited the water instantly, covering the squid in fire. It let out a loud, cruel hiss and released itself from the boat. Instead of submerging back to the depths, it panicked and did the only thing it could think of to combat this new danger; the squid released its stomach acid into the water.

The acid burned into the bottles of acetylene that was still attached to it, causing the gas to release directly into the fiery water. An explosion flared up over the side of the boat as it started a chain reaction that began exploding the rest of the bottles in the water around the squid. Trapped in a minefield, the monster could do nothing but squeal in pain as four of the bottles exploded from underneath it, turning it into a thousand pieces of chum.

The explosion rocked the side of the boat, shattering the windows in the wheelhouse and shearing off the crab block that hung over the rail, sending it flying into the bait shredder. Mike and John threw their bodies over Kyle to protect him from the shards of glass and pieces of flaming squid that were falling from the sky. After several minutes, the last piece finally fell.

Mike and John helped the greenhorn to his feet and stood on the open deck as they looked around. Small patches of fire littered the deck as the men raced to grab buckets and extinguish them. After the last fire was finally out, they walked to the railing and looked at the aftermath of the explosion.

The right side of the boat was completely scorched from the fire, black burn streaks ran up and down the hull. Most of the paint was gone and indentations in the metal from the weight of the squid made the boat look like it had been through a side on collision.

"Do you guys see any sign of him?" John asked them as he tried to find any evidence of Captain Wilder in the water.

Mike scanned the water as he blocked the blinding sun with his hand. Small areas of the water still burned from the fuel, but from what he could see, there was no sign of the captain.

Suddenly, Kyle yelled and pointed with his hand at a spot in the water fifty feet from the boat.

Lying on the surface was a twenty foot tentacle that was slowly sinking, and at the end of it, Captain Wilder's hat was stuck to one of the suction cups. The men watched for several minutes as the hat finally sank below the surface, falling into the depths of the seabed.

"Well, he's gone," Mike said as he stared into the water, mesmerized by the stillness of it. "Let's get an inventory of what we have left, and let's get the hell out of here, guys."

John walked to the railing and tossed a water-soaked cigarette pack into the water. "Good riddance, the crazy bastard tried to get us killed out here, and for what? Money? We lost an entire crew for that man, and he got the easiest way out."

Mike walked over to him and snapped him back to reality. "That doesn't matter anymore, what matters now is we make it back alive. John, I need you to go down to the engine room and make sure our last engine is in shape to get us back."

He turned to Kyle and gave him a job. "I need you to go to the galley and see how much food we have left, get a count of everything edible. I'm gonna assume by how slow we're gonna be going it'll be a while before we make it back to port. After killing that creature I'd hate if the thing that kills me was starvation."

"You got it, Mike." Kyle started walking toward the ready room door when he heard Mike call his name. He turned and looked at the new captain of *The Restless*.

"You're one hell of a crewmate, Kyle. For being your first time out, you did a hell of a job. I don't know what's gonna be in store for us when we make it back, but if you want to stick around for a while, we could sure use your help."

Kyle smiled at Mike before he opened the door. "I don't plan on going anywhere, Captain. I'm with you guys till the end." Kyle walked through the door and headed into the galley.

John walked over to Mike and smiled before smacking him on the back. "He's a good kid, boss. We're lucky he made it through this whole thing. Hell, we're lucky any of us made it." John unwrapped a fresh pack of cigarettes and lit one of them in his mouth. "So, what happens when we get back into town? How the hell do we explain all this to the police?"

"I don't know," Mike answered. "I'll have to think of that on our way there. Good thing is I should have plenty of time to come up with something. I doubt they would even believe us if we told them the truth, other than just us on the boat, we don't have any evidence that that thing even existed."

John took a drag from his cigarette. "Well, we could probably just say there was an accident, that'd at least be believable." He blew the smoke out before flicking the butt into the water. "I'll be down below, get us the hell out of here, Mike."

John walked down to the engine room while Mike made his way up to the wheelhouse. Picking up the phone, Mike called the galley to see how much food they had left.

"Well, it's mostly good news, Captain. We have plenty of canned food left and still have a lot of food left in the freezer. I'd say we have close to a month's supply of food, but that's if we ration it."

"Ok, thanks, Kyle. After you're finished with that, make sure everything is secured out on deck. We're gonna be heading back as soon as we get the go ahead from John in the engine room," Mike instructed him.

"Will do, Cap," Kyle answered before hanging up the phone.

******

Down in the engine room, John finished the last of his preparations for the trip home. He put fresh oil in their remaining engine and checked the pressure. Seeing it was in the green, he called Mike and told him they were ready to get under way. Once he hung up the phone, he gave the room one more check to ensure he hadn't forgotten anything. Walking out of the room, he left the light on and closed the door behind him.

Once he reached the deck, John helped Kyle finish securing their few remaining pots and cleaned up the last of the debris that was still there. Kyle walked to the bait station intercom and informed Mike that the last of the preparations were finished.

In the wheelhouse, Mike started the engine, praying that it would turn on. With a groan, it slowly came alive, and Mike plotted their course home into the boat's GPS system. He activated the throttle and steered a course for home. He picked up the mic for the deck speaker and spoke into it.

"This is Captain Mike Caden of the fishing vessel *The Restless*, let's go home, guys." He hung the mic back into its harness and began the journey back to port.

PROLOGUE

One week later

Mike sat in the chair in the wheelhouse, rubbing his eyes from sleep deprivation. One perk to working out on deck was being able to move around and get the blood pumping in his body. But up here, all he could do was sit and stare out into the sea. He checked their heading in the computer and noticed they had arrived at the site where they had laid the first set of crab pots. Looking down at his watch, it read just after twelve in the afternoon.

Something caught his eye as he looked back up to the window, something in the water. He squinted his eyes and saw something orange floating on the surface, maybe a buoy that had been lost. Mike debated just leaving it there but as he thought about it, this boat was his now, and he would need to save money any way he could to pay for the repairs. He picked up the phone and woke the crew.

"Uhh, yeah. What's up, boss?" John muttered, waking up from a nap.

"Hey, sorry to bother you, John, but there's something out in the water. I wanted to know if you and Kyle could go take a look at what it is."

Tension spiked in John's voice. "What kind of thing?"

Mike laughed as he could tell what the concern was about. "Don't worry, nothing large and covered in tentacles. It looks like it might be one of our buoys. Grab a net or something and bring it on board, would ya?"

"Can do, Captain Caden... Hey, I like the sound of that." John chuckled as the receiver moved away from his mouth." Hey Kyle, wake up. The boss man wants us to clean up some trash out of the water. If you beat me out there, I'll make you a full share deckhand!"

The receiver hung up.

Mike chuckled to himself as he imagined the greenhorn sliding all over the galley trying to beat John outside. Within three minutes, he saw John burst through the door out on deck, Kyle right on his heels.

Mike picked up the mic. "Close but no cigar, Kyle, looks like you're still on the bottom of the totem pole." He laughed as he put the mic onto the harness and laid back in the chair as he watched them put a long pole net over the side of the rail.

He could see John was struggling to lift the net back over the side. Whatever was inside it couldn't have been a pot buoy. Mike's curiosity increased the longer it took for John and Kyle to hoist the net. Maybe there was some pot debris that was still attached to it.

Finally, the two deckhands lifted the net over the railing, and the orange object sat in the netting. They huffed and puffed as the net dropped onto the deck, and by Mike's view, it had come down with force. Whatever it was, it was heavy. The two men just stood over the object and stared at it, not moving an inch. Mike got onto the intercom and asked them what it was.

John finally walked to the bait station speaker, "Mike, you're gonna wanna come see this."

Mike let the microphone hang as he quickly got out of his chair and ran down to the deck.

******

Questions swirled in Mike's head as he tried to comprehend what he was looking at. He knew what it was, but at the same time couldn't believe it. The orange, slime-covered ball sitting on the deck was the size of a bowling ball, and pulsed almost as if it had a heartbeat. He bent down and looked into the center of it and could see the outlines of a thin body, with what looked like eight tiny legs coming from the bottom of it.

"What is it?" Kyle asked them.

"It's an egg," Mike said coldly.

John shifted where he was standing, obviously nervous. "No fucking way, man, we killed that thing days ago. How the hell is there an egg out here?"

Mike stood back up and walked over to a supply closet on deck and grabbed the hatchet he had used during their battle with the squid. He came back to the egg and slammed the blade down into the center of it. He hacked several times until the egg burst open and the body of an eight inch baby squid flopped onto the deck. The eye in the middle of its body looked around and tried to crawl towards John.

The last thing the squid saw was the bottom of Mike's boot as he slammed it through its head. "'Cause there's another one out there."

"Bullshit," John shot back. "There's no way there's another one of those things out here."

Kyle heard some kind of noise coming from the water and walked over to see what it was. His jaw dropped. "Ugh, you guys need to come see this."

They walked over to him and looked out into the sea. Hundreds of orange balls began floating to the surface one by one; they were completely surrounded by eggs.

"What are we gonna do now?" Kyle asked, picking the hatchet up out of the broken egg.

Mike made a straight path for the wheelhouse. "We're going back to port, now."

"Well, we know that, boss, but what are we gonna do about these things?" John asked, pointing to the water. "Or the other giant squid that's out here?"

Mike stopped in his tracks and turned around to them. "Let's worry about getting back in one piece first. When we get back, we've got work to do. We're gonna make these things pay for what they did to our friends."

John smiled as he saw the fire in their new captain's eyes. "I like the sound of that, boss, count me in."

"Me too," Kyle interjected. "What are we gonna do for a crew though?"

Mike smiled as he made one more dash for the wheelhouse. "Don't worry about that, I've got some friends that owe me a couple favors. Get some sleep, guys, we're gonna be pretty busy here soon. This boat is gonna get some modifications that'll make that trap look like a fun house."

John smiled. "Now we're talking. This time, we get an even playing field."

They walked back inside and commenced their journey back to town.

THE END

Check out other great

Sea Monster Novels!

Michael Cole

SCAR

Scar is a killing machine. Born from DNA spliced between the extinct Megalodon and modern day Great White, he has a viciousness that transcends time. His evil is reflected in his eyes, his savagery in his two-inch serrated teeth, his ruthlessness in his trail of death. After escaping captivity, the killer shark travels to the island community Cross Point, where prey is in abundance. With an insatiable appetite, heightened senses, and skin impervious to bullets, Scar kills everything that crosses his path. His reign of terror puts him at war with the island sheriff, Nick Piatt. With the body count rising, Nick vows to protect his island community from the vicious threat. With the aid of a marine biologist, a rookie deputy, and a bad-tempered fisherman, Nick leads a crusade against Scar, as well as the ruthless scientist who created him.

Rick Chesler

HOTEL MEGALODON

An underwater luxury hotel on a gorgeous tropical island is set for an extravagant opening weekend with the world watching. The only thing standing in the way of a first-rate experience for the jet-setting VIPs is an unscrupulous businessman and sixty feet of prehistoric shark. As the underwater complex is besieged by a marauding behemoth, newly minted marine biologist Coco Keahi must face off against the ancient predator as it rises from the deep with a vengeance. Meanwhile, a human monster has decided he would be better off if Coco were one of the creature's victims.

Check out other great

Sea Monster Novels!

Edward J. McFadden III

SHADOW OF THE ABYSS

Out of the past comes an immense horror. An ancient creature that must feed its voracious hunger. A massive landslide on Grand Bahama Bank sends a thirty-foot wave traveling at 150MPH toward the east coast of Florida, and the tsunami drags in something horrible from the depths of the Mid-Atlantic Ridge rift valley. Now a monster roams Florida's east coast and its shallows, searching for prey. Matthew "Splinter" Woods lives in Sailfish Haven. He's a washed-out Navy SEAL who lives off the grid on his dilapidated boat and has withdrawn from society rather than face his demons. But when his ex-girlfriend, charter boat captain Lenah Brisbee, comes to him for help, Splinter gets drawn into a battle that pits him against the strongest enemy he's ever faced as he races against time to find the monster before it turns the waters he loves blood red.

Eric S. Brown

PIRANHA

The rains came, flooding the sleepy, little town of Sylva. Sheriff Hanson never thought that he would be fighting a battle to survive against real life monsters. . .but with the waters came flesh eating, hungry creatures that swept through Sylva's streets like locusts, devouring everyone in their path.

Check out other great

Sea Monster Novels!

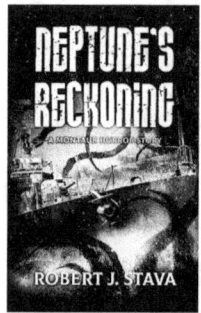

Robert J. Stava

NEPTUNES RECKONING

At the easternmost end of Long Island lies a seaside town known as Montauk. Ground Zero on the Eastern seaboard for all manner of conspiracy theories involving it's hidden Cold War military base, rumors of time-travel experiments and alien visitors... For renowned Naval historian William Vanek it's the where his grandfather's ship went down on a Top Secret mission during WWII code-named "Neptune's Reckoning". Together with Marine Biologist Daniel Cheung and disgraced French underwater explorer Arnaud Navarre, he's about to discover the truth behind the urban legends: a nightmare from beyond space and time that has been reawakened by global warming and toxic dumping, a nightmare the government tried to keep submerged. Neptune's Reckoning. Terror knows no depth

Bestselling collection

DEAD BAIT

A husband hell-bent on revenge hunts a Wereshark... A Russian mail order bride with a fishy secret... Crabs with a collective consciousness... A vampire who transforms into a Candiru... Zombie piranha...Bait that will have you crawling out of your skin and more. Drawing on horror, humor with a helping of dark fantasy and a touch of deviance, these 19 contemporary stories pay homage to the monsters that lurk in the murky waters of our imaginations. If you thought it was safe to go back in the water... Think Again!